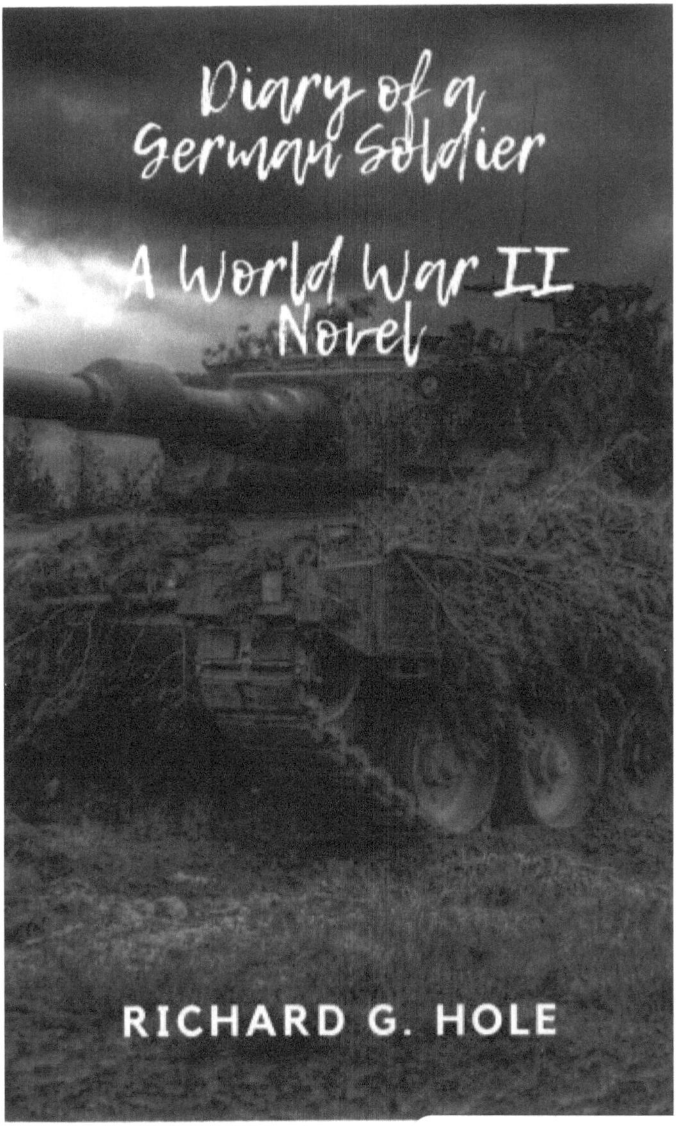

Diary of a German Soldier

A World War II Novel

RICHARD G. HOLE

Diary of a German Soldier
A World War II Novel

1

Richard G. Hole

World War II

SUMMARY

This offensive that we are about to begin can, perhaps, attenuate the suffocating armor that surrounds us. God forbid.

Otherwise, our beautiful country, the most beautiful country in the world and until recently, alas, the strongest, will know the boot of the invader.

Since Napoleon's time we have never been so close to it, nor do I think we will ever be in future centuries, because this war will have to be the last of wars.

That, at least, is what the allies say, although do they even believe it?

Diary of a German Soldier is a story belonging to the World War II collection, a series of war novels developed in World War II

DIARY OF A GERMAN SOLDIER

FIRST PART

December, 6.

We have been in this place for seven days now. Seven days of inactivity seems like a lot if you think about everything we have done so far, but to the troops and to us they have seemed very short. We rested.

I have written we rest. He should have said that we prepare, because that is what we are doing: preparing for the onslaught. Anyone who thought that Germany was already defeated, bled, and now saw how the trains loaded with troops and material arrive in this region of the Eifel (I have counted up to a hundred newspapers), might think that he was wrong, that the country still retains its force.

But let's not fool ourselves. These troops are the last embers of the fire. For the first time since 1918 the enemies are close to our borders. Here in front of us. They are close to our country, they surround us. They have already reached the Saarland and threaten Cologne. The Russians are approaching Budapest with forced marches ... the English are back in Greece ... God, how I hate having to write all this. The pen refuses to do so.

On the other hand, this offensive that we are about to begin can, perhaps, attenuate the suffocating armor that surrounds us. God forbid. Otherwise, our beautiful country, the most beautiful country in the world and until recently, alas, the strongest, will know the boot of the invader. Since Napoleon's time we have never been so close to it, nor do I think we will ever be in future centuries, because this war will have to be the last of wars.

That, at least, is what the allies say, although do they even believe it?

But I am not a writer or historian. I am simply a soldier. Therefore, this is the diary of a soldier. A diary that I write for myself because otherwise I would go crazy. No more rhetoric: hard facts. I leave it to others to faithfully transcribe the causes of the war, the reasons for our defeats.

The facts?

I, Ulrich Tagger, Major of the Second Division of the German Fifth Panzer Army, am in the vicinity of Pronsfield, with my division, with my Army. Here are our faithful «Panthers», our faithful «Tigers», oiled, clean, supplied with ammunition and oil "oh, oil, how expensive you are and how little we see you now, since we have lost those splendid Romanian fields". Yes, we are ready. So that?

Just yesterday I was talking to an "aide" of Von Manteuffel, commander of the Fifth Panzer Army.

"Tagger" tells me ". They still cannot agree.

"In the name of... Haller, what's wrong with you?

"That, they cannot agree. The Führer has said one thing, Von Rundstedt says another, Model says another and I say that if we don't hurry we won't be able to do it.

"Do what, Haller?

Haller, tall, thin as wicker, with a fine Prussian head and dark hair, looks around.

"Isn't that Hagen monster around?

"No, no" I answer impatiently "What do you have to name Hagen for now?

"I would not like you to hear what I am going to say" Hagen "I say a little stiffly", he is one of my best officers. Or rather: the best of my tank bosses.

"I know, I know, and I would be the last to deny his merits; but the last time it occurred to me to speak in front of him of a conversation I had heard from the general, he repeated it in a tavern before a group of officers, adding some comments of his own making.

I try not to smile. I remember the case: Hagen said that if a flock of monkeys want the same peanut to eat, one of them will get it, and this one will probably be the strongest, not the smartest.

"Forget Hagen," I say. " Now he is not here, but in the village, probably.

"Making love to some ...

"Well, the point is, he's not here. What were you going to tell me?

"Tagger, there are two different opinions on what we should do. One, that of the Führer, another that of Rundstedt. The Führer wants to throw the Americans and English into the sea immediately. Right now. Already. Rundstedt and Model prefer a series of flakes in the North, which could undo that spearhead with which the Americans threaten Cologne. It could be done without losing a lot of people.

"If I say ". I have looked at the map many times and, although I am not a staff officer, I know what you mean. To launch the Americans and the English into the sea, you have to attack from there, towards Antwerp.

"Exactly. The allies have not yet commissioned the port of Antwerp. If we can get to it, we will have served them a bone that they probably won't be able to gnaw. The Führer's plan is not bad; but will we have enough strength to carry it out? Rundstedt and Model believe not. And that's the situation. In the end you will see how, anyway, that is the plan that will be carried out, to attack towards Antwerp.

"Yes" I answer. " The strongest monkey will have eaten the peanut.

"Don't repeat phrases like that. And if you're trying to say that the Führer isn't the smartest ...

That is the situation. But her resolution depends on stronger and more capable shoulders than mine. Whether we attack towards Antwerp, splitting the Ardennes and the Belgian plain, or if we dedicate ourselves to host the English and the Americans in the North, my job will be the same: to slip into my «Tiger», put on my helmet and guide the machine trying to destroy as many English "Centurions" as possible without destroying me.

And that will be what I do: fulfill my obligation. I am a soldier.

December, 7.

Haller was right. Hagen is a spawn, a force of nature, a sacred bull, the great genital! Is it not enough for the concerns inherent in a war in which Germany risks everything, its very existence, but rather that it has to look for accessory complications?

Dieter Hagen is my best captain. And surely the best captain in the division, and probably the best tank captain in the Fifth Army. That is not denied by anyone. That is said by the others in a low voice, and by himself in a very loud voice. On that, then, we all agree.

But in other things ...

In other things he is a true devil, as imponderable as a typhoon in the Pacific.

With women, of course. And, in many cases, with men.

If life consisted solely of battles, Hagen would fight, he would receive an Iron Cross with oak leaves every morning, and everyone would be glad to have a hero by his side.

But it so happens that even in war there are moments of peace, of tranquility, while the next attack is being prepared or the next withdrawal is organized. And it is in those moments that Hagen sticks out the satyr's furry ear.

And how it appears!

I'm not going to say that all skirts are good for him. No, not at all; that would be insulting him, seriously injuring him. Not; what happens is that he is able to find the "best skirt" wherever he goes. It will be useless for that woman to be buried at the bottom of a cellar, perched on the top of the most leafy tree. Hagen will discover her, make love to her and seduce her as surely as the sun rises daily in the East and sets in the West.

We have fought together in Italy, in France and now here, in our own country. Everywhere he has done the same. And I know he has done it before in Greece, in North Africa. If he is now only a captain and not a colonel at thirty and after five years of war, it is due to two causes: The first, his long-standing habit of speaking ill of superiors and command. The second, to women. Without those two facets of his character, it is almost certain that now he would be the one giving me orders instead of receiving them from me.

I like women, of course, because I am a young, healthy and normal man. But from there to find reasons for seduction both in a Libyan girl with the color of nutmeg, as in an Italian matron with mahogany hair, in a stylized Parisian with saffron hair or in a Belgian with porcelain eyes ..., there is a lot of distance.

Well, that distance is covered by Hagen, if necessary, in two jumps. If they had assigned him to Russia, from which he has been freed on many occasions by the edge of a razor, the census of children in that accursed country would have increased by a good number of units.

But his latest feat has pushed the limits. Yes, it has surpassed them because this is not Greece, or Libya, not even France or Italy, This is Germany, the Vaterland.

Good German laws still apply here. Why the hell can't that man just sit still and leave his hormones alone?

I'm going to relate it. After all, and after having had the daily meeting with the Brigade commander, after the routine inspection of the machines, after verifying that the men have not lost a single piece of discipline, I hardly have anything to do.

"Yes, I relate it.

Oberst Pieck is the first to blast me. He is the head of the regiment and his chest is overcrowded with medals.

"Tagger" he told me. Have you heard of your captain's latest feat?

"It is not" my "captain, colonel," I replied respectfully. " He is "one" of the captains of the Regiment.

"Oberst" Pieck, who is barely two years older than me, has put on the face of "don't give me distinctions and stick to the bare facts."

"I don't want to find out until the complaint is officially made: but Hagen has done something that can lead directly to a military court. Which would surely lead to it, unless the situation is not enough to deprive us of a captain.

"From one of the best captains" I answer, always with the same respect.

"It's okay. From one of the best captains, if you like; but at the same time one of the most fractious, compromising, and corrosive elements that can occur in the German Army.

I wait for it to be explained, if you want to. Doesn't want to, apparently.

"Wait, if you haven't found out yet, and you'll see if you find one of your usual excuses for him then.

I am very careful not to tell him that other times he has found excuses himself. Like, for example, when in Reims, Hagen took him out of a burning car, with almost absolute risk to his own life, and carried him in his arms for an hour until he found our lines again.

And with him in his arms, because Pieck was passed out, he fought a duel with French resisters with pistol shots.

No, those things cannot be said to a colonel. Let him remember them.

It was Gefreiter Behme who explained it to me half an hour later. The corporal is usually Hagen's Sancho Panza. He follows him everywhere, gives him advice that he himself is quick to refuse, and covers him in those adventures in which it is necessary to use four hands, four feet and two pistols. In his spare time he is your chariot gunner.

'Corporal' I say to Behme, who whistles as he holsters the Hagen's 'Tiger' ". You are going to explain to me what new trouble the captain has gotten himself into.

"How, sir commander?" He asks, making a stupid face.

"Behme, I don't want to waste time. I want to know what the captain has done. And I want to know "for you."

His face continues to be a display of the most concentrated stupidity.

"I can't understand what the commander means.

"You will understand if I arrest you. Come on, Behme, you know the captain won't find out from me that it was you who told me. You know, don't you?

"Yes, sir commander" is what the rascal is waiting for. Assurances that Hagen won't kick her out with him as a whistleblower.

"I talked.

"Well ... it is, in a way, the burgomaster.

"In 'a way', Behme?

"This... yes, sir commander. Seems that if.

"The mayor of Pronsfield, Behme?

"Yes, sir commander.

I know her. A woman in her thirties, with butter-colored hair, a Nordic Juno in whom Nature placed the extraordinary whim of two almost southern eyes, dark, bright and extremely inviting. I also know the burgomaster, a two-meter-tall lout, with legs like tree trunks and a sour character.

"What has the captain done, Behme?" I ask chilled.

He looks at me with the stereotypical innocence in his fox pupils,

"Mr. Commander, perhaps Mr. Captain Hagen would explain better than I ...

"Speak up, Behme!

"Well ... We can say, commander, that the burgomaster found Captain Hagen in the company of the burgomaster and ...

"Holy God!

The morning is freezing. From the Taunus, crossing the Moselle valley, a cold wind comes to us that predicts snow for soon. But it is not cold that I shudder.

"What happened, Behme?

He acts like a swimmer who throws himself headfirst into icy waves.

"Mr. Captain Hagen shot down Mr. Burgomaster and beat him up.

It's not hard for me to believe it. That's very Hagen. After seducing the wife, hit the husband. In similar cases, the full pension is taken.

I don't wait any longer and I address myself to the Division's General Staff, taking advantage of the fact that a "DKW" had that address. We have the machines hidden in a thick forest of chestnut and beech trees, wrapped in camouflage fabrics. Many times we have seen the great formations of Allied bombers and their photographic planes pass over us and they have never even suspected that there, below them, there are 150 tanks ready to attack as soon as they are given the order.

The Division General Staff is in Pronsfield, the Army in Bitburg. I was interested in the first of the two.

Everywhere an extraordinary activity reigns. As I already said, trains arrive daily in the Eifel in huge numbers, sometimes more than a hundred. Thus, by eye, and from what I have seen, I can calculate that no less than twenty divisions must be concentrating here. Everything, under the nose of the allied planes. It's possible? As a German I am proud. Overdue? Ah! You will see.

Right now we feel its thunderous sound above the low clouds. Perhaps they return from razing some of the cities of our country, from vilely destroying thousands of children, from gutting women and the elderly. The driver of the "DKW" raises his fist in the air and curses, very pale.

In the General Staff of the Division, housed in a former palace of aristocrats, there is a lot of activity. Cars, motorcycles with soldiers who carry parts from one place to another, fill the esplanade in front of the Plaza Mayor. Radio and telegraph buzz insistently.

In what was once a ballroom of some former marquis or baron, the nerve center of operations is installed. Officers study the maps, receive the parts, and plot their plans over and over again. In a way I find myself a little lost there; but fortunately I have good friends. One of them is Colonel Von Simmenthal, who was with me in the Gymnasium when we were students, back at the Schleswig.

Taking advantage of a moment when he seems to be free, I approach him.

Hello, Tagger. What's up? Any news with the machines?

"Nothing, Mr. Officer" I say respectfully, as there are many officers listening to us and familiarities are not proper in those cases.

"Did you want something?

"It's about Hagen, Colonel.

"Ah, Hagen ...

His eyes gleam behind the air-mounted lenses, an exact copy of those worn by the Aeichführer Himmler.

"You've gotten into trouble, haven't you?

"I don't know very well, Colonel.

He realizes that I don't want to speak to others. He takes me by the arm and leads me to the canteen.

"Let's have some coffee," he says.

We sink our mustaches into that hideous mixture that is made up of acorn juice and burnt cloth, sparingly sweetened with saccharin.

"Simmenthal" I say ". What have they done with Hagen?

"But, dear Tagger, I am a Colonel of General Staff, not an officer of the watch.

"What I want to say is that Hagen is my best man and that I am not prepared to do without him in the event that we get going.

"Well well; But, what can i do?

He looks at me, apparently puzzled. I am not fooled by his innocent appearance.

"I want you to get him out of where he is. You have appointed the officer of the watch. That means you are under arrest.

"Yes I think so.

"Well then, I want you to speak to the general if necessary and have Hagen's arrest lifted.

"Man, Tagger, don't you think you're asking too much?

"Not.

I hope my tone sounds uncompromising enough. Seems that if.

"I will do what i can. I know that Hagen is ... Well, well, I'll do what I can.

"Get me a pass to see it.

They bring it to me in a short time.

Hagen has been placed in a room with a well-locked door. That means that, as usual, he has not given his word of honor not to leave the building.

The duty officer accompanies me.

"They have filed a complaint against him, haven't they?" I ask. What kind of complaint?

His eyes shine, like Simmenthal's. It seems that this is the reaction he provokes in all of Hagen's adventures.

"Aggression to the administrative authority.

So they have not wanted to bring out the mayor.

He opens the door to the room and lets me pass.

December, 7. Later

Hagen is sitting on a cot, smoking, his tunic unbuttoned. He looks at me as he walks in and winks at me. As soon as the officer of the watch leaves, I spread my legs and put my thumbs in my belt.

"Well, you piece of animal, what have you done now?

"Didn't they tell you?

"I want you to tell me ..." you. "

You can imagine from what I have written about Hagen that he is not an ordinary guy. It could not be a man who takes just one look to upset a woman, five seconds to find the best way to attack and destroy a tank of greater tonnage than his own, and ten minutes to remove an armored regiment from a field. in which it cannot maneuver well to place it in another where it can function with all the advantages.

He is tall, with anchor shoulders and narrow hips. As far as I know, there is not a single southerner among his ancestors; but he has dark hair and brown eyes. His hands are big and hairy; his neck, solid; his legs, straight as columns.

"Do you know Ana?" He asks me.

"Yes, I know her. "I know" she's another man's wife, and that you damn funny monkey should have thought so.

"Shut up now. You asked me and I answer you. Do you want to hear it or not?

"Speak, damn it!

"Well that. If you know her, what else can I add? I told her she had lovely eyes and she put her arms around my neck. Her husband arrived at that moment.

"You are not going to tell me that you were at his house at night, just to tell him that he had lovely eyes.

He looks at me mockingly, and closes his mouth.

"Well, what did you do to that poor man?

"Stop him from doing anything to me.

"What did you do to him?"

"I put him in a horizontal position. Some gossipers add that I kicked it, but I can't remember that detail. There are certain gaps in my memory, Ulrich.

"Do you know that hitting a mayor is not as innocent a thing as drinking a liter of wine? You know?

"I have a slight idea about it.

"And that that can take you in front of the Military Court?

"That, already ...

He shrugs.

"Look" I say approaching him. Very serious things are being prepared. Because of this we will ensure that nothing happens to you ... for the moment, because of this dirty task. Otherwise, I can assure you that I would let you rot in this room until a court assigned you elsewhere.

He looks at me strangely.

"And how do you know, Ulrich, that I have not done this dirty job to avoid being involved in those grave events you speak of?

I feel the blood run cold in my veins when I hear it. Can not be. It is impossible. Dieter Hagen could not have done such a thing. My ears are deceiving me.

I can hardly manage to stammer:

"What the hell do you ...?

He gets up and slaps me on the shoulder.

"Come on, come on, Ulrich, don't make that scared face. I have not made an excuse not to go to the front, if that is what terrifies you. All I did was get a little careless. I also had no wish for that animal to find me comforting his wife. It was simply my bad star that brought him in when Ana's ear was very close to my mouth.

I retreat, somewhat reassured. I myself, many times, in the course of the last few months, have surprised myself thinking that I was already fed up with the war and that all I wanted was to be able to rest calmly, somewhere, and spend the rest of my days without having to continually plan the best way to destroy a fellow man of mine. But I have managed to drive away those bad thoughts, as is my duty, and replace them with the idea that if we become demoralized, what will become of our country? I must not give shelter, not for a single moment, to such defeatist thoughts.

"We will do what we can for you," I tell him. But if you leave here, I will make sure that you do not move from my side again, and I will not take my eyes off you for a single moment.

I slam the door shut, while he stands there, grinning. That damned womanizer knows well that we need it, that if every man capable of lifting a rifle and pulling the trigger is necessary for our country, he, who knows how to do many more things, is essential.

At the palace gate I find the officer of the guard talking to a group of people. The burgomaster is there, and her husband is there too.

What put you in a horizontal position? Ha! The mayor's face reveals the traces of the beating he suffered to the most blinded eyes. He might as well have tripped over the chains of a tank on a dark night; such are the marks that Hagen's fists have left on his brute face.

And the mayor? Beneath her gray cloth coat, which is not enough to hide her splendid forms as a woman in the prime of her life, she appears smiling, her eyes narrowed, her red mouth ajar to reveal two rows of polished teeth.

Her husband talks to the officer, waving his hands. Between his purplish lips the dent of a tooth is black, probably snatched away when he was trying to defend an honor that he had no interest in being defended.

Finally the woman takes her husband by the arm, says something to him in a low voice and they turn. There are already many soldiers and some countrymen, gathered, watching the couple with ironic interest.

December, 8.

Today, Reverend Finstenmeier said a campaign mass for being a very prominent Catholic holiday. Our Bavarian and Austrian soldiers have attended in great numbers.

Meanwhile, bad news comes from everywhere. The Russians are forty kilometers from Budapest, and today they gave us the news that the English have occupied Ravenna, in Italy. Follow the fence.

Hagen has not returned, and I have not been able to travel to Pronsfield. After all, my duty is here in the camouflage camp. But I have spoken to "Oberst" Pieck, who always seems to be delighted to be the bearer of bad news. He was the one who told me about Budapest.

"Apparently, the mayor wants justice at all costs" he told me when he made sure that I knew the story. " And it doesn't surprise me. Hagen cannot behave as if he is on conquered ground. This is not Italy.

"No, Mr. Colonel" I respond respectfully.

"If it weren't because we need him ... Man, I consider that sleeping with a thirty-year-old woman is not a crime; but you must have some respect for the mocked husband. Don't you think Tagger?

"Indeed, Colonel, and I have made it known to Captain Hagen.

"In the event the matter is postponed, Captain Hagen will be under your watch, Tagger, and you will be responsible for what you do. I want this to be well understood.

"Yes, Colonel.

I have to answer 'yes, Colonel,' but what you are ordering me to do is take direct responsibility for the sirocco not causing damage to a Bedouin caravan in the desert. I can threaten Hagen with my surveillance, but can I hold myself responsible? The load will be heavy.

Not that I'm too excited about the idea of starting to advance with the tanks in front of the enemy, but almost, almost, I wish it. At least I know that during the action, Hagen watches himself.

December, 9.

The Americans are advancing on the Saar front. Nothing is known yet about the offense. The hours go by slower than ever.

I am writing in one of the rooms of the farm where the brigade has the liaison office installed. A dense fog, colder than if we were in Greenland, has descended on the countryside.

We drink brandy and brandy to warm up. I have had a very heavy guard, since at night the alarms have sounded. Hundreds of allied aircraft have passed over us. The roar of its engines was like the beating of a giant double bass. Even the earth shook.

Fortunately they have no idea that we are here. Otherwise...

Hagen? He continues in the Division's General Staff. I have heard from you through Gefreiter Behme. Assuming the bloody corporal would somehow manage to see his captain, I have brought him cigarettes and brandy. When he returns, the corporal tells me that the captain is well and that he has immediately honored both.

"Apparently" he continues, "Mayor Wald has said that he would withdraw the accusation if the captain apologized to him personally.

In saying it, the corporal did not look at me. He seemed very interested in the hovering of a royal finch.

"What do you mean? Who is it that gave you this news, Behme?

"Well ... no one, in particular, sir commander. I've heard it somewhere.

"Where? To who?

"Over there, sir commander. I consider myself incapable of remembering where or to whom.

I would not be surprised if this bergante has been mixed in the matter. He is quite capable of doing so on the orders of his captain.

December, 10.

Taking advantage of a short break, during which, apparently, my presence was not necessary, I have gone to Pronsfield, five kilometers away from where we are camped.

I have learned from one of my many excellent friends that the indictment could indeed be dropped. In this case it was a commander who was with me in Paris, in the same hospital, who told me. He's the secretary to the military judge, Colonel Weiberg, so you must know well.

"I'm going to tell you in confidence that Mayor Wald looks scared. Can you believe it?

"I think so.

"It is not that Colonel Weiberg is eager to carry out a trial against Hagen; But if you are pressured, you will have to. We have spoken with the burgomaster and his wife ... By the way, Tagger, have you noticed what piece of woman?

"Yes. But, going back to Hagen ...

What eyes, what legs and what ...; but, hell, if you've seen her I have no need to make your apology. I assure you that I would not have minded in any way that I, too, had undertaken a small conquest of her on my own. But things don't seem too good for a love offense.

"Going back to Hagen ..." I repeat patiently.

"Well, it seems ... and note that I apparently say, 'Herr' Wald has gotten some hints about what might happen to him if the trial went ahead and he seems eager to settle the matter. As long as Hagen makes excuses for him.

"In public?" He asked, horrified. I know Hagen won't do that even if his neck is tied into a hemp rope.

"Man no. Gee, the thing is not so bad. I mean from the point of view of a man like Wald, little more than a peasant. "Herr" Wald will be content to let his administrations know that an officer had apologized, even if they did not see him doing so. "Herr" Wald is a patriot in his own way. He realizes that we are at war and that officers must have some privileges.

"Maybe that could be done," I say thoughtfully.

"Well, in that case everything would work out. But I'd like to know who it is that has been scaring Wald. Perhaps his wife. I have found it very capable of doing it.

I think of Corporal Behme and his devotion to Hagen, but I don't consider it my duty to inform him. After all, he is the clerk of the examining magistrate, not me.

I ask to see Hagen, but they tell me it can't be.

December, 11.

Nothing in particular except that, as troops continue to arrive in the Eifel, we are going to have to climb on top of each other. Today I have seen two trains with soldiers coming from the Russian front. Things have to go badly for them to remove troops from there, with the brutal pressure of the Soviet "verdammters" on all fronts. They come with the torn clothes, the hallucinated eyes and the terror in the pupils. I smoked a cigarette with one of the officers, but they are silent as dead. They don't want to mention "that."

December, 12.

The Russians advance northeast of Budapest. How bad everything is going! Thousands of allied planes have bombed the homeland. I imagine my old mother over there at the Schleswig will be reasonably safe. There is nothing there that can tempt those beasts that bomb a military shipyard as well as a school. It has been some time, almost thirty days, that I have not received a letter from him. The radio mentions the bombings with great circumspection. He doesn't want us to get demoralized, obviously.

Ah, there is news. We have Hagen back here with us. He arrived this morning, in time to dispatch half a bottle of brandy that I had saved for a better occasion. He has behaved as if nothing had happened. Officers have surrounded him, asking questions; but he has gotten them out of the way with a timely joke. When we were alone I asked him when they released him and he tells me that it was last night.

"Where have you been so far?" I asked him.

"You could never imagine it. At Burgomaster Wald's, drinking a bottle of Rhine wine with him and "Frau" burgomaster. I went to make excuses, and I already stayed for dinner.

As he tells me, his brown eyes look at me sarcastically. Fool me? No, this devil is not fooling me. He has, indeed, God lives.

And if the burgomaster has not discreetly withdrawn so that he and his wife can say goodbye with affection ... There are things that one does not understand nor will I ever understand, because the truth is that all my thoughts regarding Hagen are slightly tinged with envy.

There are men who, .., who should have been born in another century, in the sixteenth, for example, and he is one of them. The cloak of "condottiero" would have suited him, and the right of life and death over all the women he could conquer with his sword.

But ... did Hagen really need all those things? Don't you get everything you want ... now, in the twentieth century?

In distributing the gifts, Nature is excessively lavish with some people, and very stingy with others. Hagen is one of the first. I, of the second. Can you fight Fate?

December, 13,

The dance is going to start from one moment to the next.

I smell it. I am a veteran and I guess those things. And like me, all the officers. The consultations between the commanders of the regiment and those of the brigade, those of the brigade with those of the division ... And the extra rations that the troops receive and which are "almost" edible ... And the ammunition trains, and the huge oil tankers that we have seen camouflaged ten kilometers to the north ...

Everything, in short, is like a mosaic that a good soldier, hardened in many battles, knows how to interpret with all correctness. We are going to go into fire.

When? If they asked me the question, I would say that maybe tomorrow ... No, not tomorrow. Day after tomorrow.

We stay all the time next to the cars, or very close to them. Permits have run out.

Today there was a distribution of cognac. The cold is extremely intense and it will surely snow from one moment to the next.

Direction of offense?

I have spoken with an artillery observation captain. He told me that between Koblenz and Bonn another armored army had taken up positions. They are SS

I have looked for "Oberst" Pieck, and when he hears me he frowns.

"An SS 'Panzer' army? It can only be the sixth. It is of recent formation. They may be good people, but I doubt they have the necessary experience.

Busy as he is, Haller, Von Manteuffel's assistant, takes a few minutes for me.

"If it is the Sixth« Panzer ». Tagger, we attack towards the Ardennes.

"Who commands that army?

"General Dietrich. "Sepp" Dietrich.

I have heard of him as a good military man, but a captain ignores many things.

"So the Führer has gotten away with it.

"I think so. How could it be otherwise? Rundstedt has screamed to death, refused to run it, and Model has ended up taking command of the operation.

And what does the general say?

For us, "the general" is and will always be the commander of the Fifth "Panzer": the "generalleutnant" von Manteuffel.

Nor did he agree. He went with Model to see ... "he lowered his voice and looks around in case someone hears us" to see Colonel General Jodl. Everything has been useless. It will be attacked by The Ardennes. With what, be prepared.

"I will be, don't hesitate.

How could he have found out? When I get to our accommodation I meet Hagen. He is bent over a map and carefully measures distances. I lean over his shoulder and see what he's doing: it's the map of the Ardennes, that hilly, forested territory straddling Belgium and Luxembourg, where we'll probably find ourselves mired in a few hours.

"What are you doing?" I asked him.

"Prior recognition, dear Ulrich.

"Why precisely on this terrain?

"Because that is where we are going to try to drive out the mestizos and the English.

"How do you know?

"Premonition, Ulrich. And you know it too. We are a pair of wise old dogs; So why are we fooling ourselves?

Your index finger is firmly planted on a name on the piano.

"Look at that crossroads there, almost in front of us. We will go there.

Leo: Bastogne. Well, it is a road junction. It is very possible that he is right. One more point on the map. One more town to occupy.

"Either way ... Let's get ready.
His eyes look at me in a strange way:
"Yes," I affirm and nod.

December, 14.

Suspension of all permits, "absolutely" all. The general has personally inspected the chariots. Surrounded by his staff he has crossed before us, his head held high, his eyes firm.

More brandy and brandy for the troops. Double portion of meat, butter and potatoes.

We are all nervous, tense. Tonight English planes have bombed Cologne. Could it be that they have not noticed our presence? They must have given it to him. From Luxembourg, the Americans press firmly. His Third Army, commanded by a clown who makes officers wear their insignia on steel helmets, pushes fiercely. Did I write "clown"? It isn't, let's be fair. It is about the man who broke Britain in two a few days after the invasion. It's called Petton or Patton. They just told me.

There is talk of evacuating the German towns from this area just in case things don't go well; but why would they go wrong? We must all have confidence. Complete confidence. We are right and right, we still have the strength ... we still have it, God lives, and we will throw them into the sea. The Führer has said so. Confidence! You have to be confident.

"So... why am I really feeling fear? The nerves?

It snows furiously.

December, 15. Night.

We attack! «Deutschland, über alles! Gott mít uns!

December, 17. Night.

This is awesome! Colossal! I write fast, my handwriting will be barely legible, but if I didn't do it now, I couldn't do it anywhere else.

We have spent two nights almost without sleep, but I have not wanted to let more time pass before writing these notes, even taking it away from the sleep that I have so well earned, like everyone else.

This is not an offensive, this is an avalanche! We have pierced the Americans like a needle pierces a light pine tree. At thirty miles an hour we have advanced, destroying everything in our path!

You had to watch those half-breeds run! Like rabbits they escaped before us. We have hardly had time to eat. Forward always forward! If this continues, we will be in front of the Meuse in a few hours, we will cross it and overflow through the Flemish plain to the sea, to Antwerp. What a great general the Führer is! What a genius! Napoleon, Alexander, Hannibal! What are you at his side? Dust! Less than dust!

The German Fifth "Panzer" Army, before which succeeding generations will be exposed, has split the American defenses in two.

I will tell the part that happened to me, naturally. What does one hour or two of sleep matter when we have Germany's salivation in view? I write feverishly, still dazed with enthusiasm, wasting German fervor.

We attack at dawn. Our division got under way with the "Tigers" leading the way and the "Panthers" behind. The first obstacle that presented itself before us were the forests of northern Luxembourg, and the snow, which fell steadily. As the roads and highways were already covered, they immediately proceeded to paint the cars white to make them less visible.

From my visor I could make out the sides of the road, lined with snowy forests. Ahead of me were two wagons leading the way, on a surveillance mission, but we didn't need her until we got very close to Clervaux.

There we ran into the first American outposts, combat groups that dispersed almost without firing a shot. We left the job of eliminating the infants who came behind us, on their trucks.

We entered Clervaux, overwhelming everything in our path. The road, the streets, were narrow, and in order not to interrupt the march we had to demolish houses, level obstacles.

On the outskirts of Clervaux, a group of American engineers had placed some anti-tank defenses. That means they weren't as ignorant of our plans as we supposed. However, their jobs had been done too lightly. We broke down the cliffs and at that moment the car in front of me ran into a mine.

It was turned into a heap of junk, its belly burst open and its boss dangling sinisterly from the tower, like a disjointed doll.

I opened fire on a vehicle, a troop transport "Chevrolet," fleeing headlong into the semi-darkness of a gray and white dawn, and I had the great satisfaction of seeing it blow up.

I told the driver to slow down. This was a field strewn with mines, and I soon saw that he had been wise. A "Panther", whose number I could not distinguish, heeled violently when he stumbled on one, and his oil reservoir exploded.

Now we had light. The flares perfectly illuminated the road and field, and I watched our wagons spread out to skirt the minefield, penetrating through the forest.

My position was almost in the center of the column. I put my skin in the hands of Almighty God and ordered to advance.

God was with me! If there were any more on the road, He guided my steps so as not to trip over them. I managed to pass and fiercely charged against a building from which we were fired with bazookas and antitank fire.

Oberst Pieck's voice echoed in my ears.

"Destroy that, Tagger! Destroy those antitanks!

I knew exactly how to do it.

Less than forty meters away, at dawn that was getting whiter and whiter, I began to shoot. My gunner, a Saxon boy of admirable cold blood, took aim and sent a smashing bullet into the house. Immediately, the second and the third. They all hit the mark. At the first, the roof flew through the air, a huge mouth opened in the facade at the second, and, finally, the third exploded in the basement of the building, probably in the basement, because everything exploded like a volcano.

I saw the khaki uniforms of the American soldiers crossing into the field.

And we continue forward.

At ten o'clock in the morning we continued to penetrate deep into the meager American defenses. Then Pieck's order came to me.

"Tagger, you have to turn south. All cars to the South.

What was that? Was the objective changed?

But when we saw Pieck's car and the direction it was taking, we realized that this was a slight deviation, on the part of the division, as the rest continued forward.

I can't write anymore. I'm falling asleep. I have to save it for another time.

December, 18.

This, more than a fight, seems a massacre. I take a moment when we have stopped to get supplies, and I am going to try to recount my impressions since yesterday he had to interrupt me.

But, above all, what a spectacle of the annihilated American battalions, taken prisoner, skewered by the bayonets of our brave riflemen who sometimes have only to get out of their trucks to pick up the enemies who surrender by the hundreds! Such a show fills with joy a German heart that for so many days was constrained by doubt and fear of the future of its homeland.

They can't beat us! We beat them in every line, Germany is saved!

Yes, I do, despite the wry looks Hagen gave me when I told him. So I let you know barely half an hour ago.

The camouflaged tanker trucks have arrived a moment ago to supply us with fuel. The sky, covered with clouds, thank God, does not allow American airplanes to do us much harm, even though we sometimes hear information and photography devices hovering above our heads, like disoriented butterflies.

According to my news, to the North, the SS "Panzer" Sixth Army is also advancing with fury and determination to divide the English and the Americans.

If we separate the two armies, the allies will turn their proud behinds and throw themselves into the sea to save themselves. France will be before our eyes again, and Germany will be saved.

What does Captain Hagen have to oppose to that?

Standing in front of his car, helmet in hand, his neck wrapped in his silk scarf, he smokes eagerly. He offers me a cigarette, while it's our turn to refuel, and we wait for Pieck to give us our orders.

The forests of the Ardennes stretch around us. A desolate place, in this harsh winter. Low hills covered with trees, charcoal kilns ...

It has stopped snowing.

"I think you are too impressionable, dear Ulrich," Hagen tells me.

"But don't you see that beyond these cursed forests is the Meuse, and behind the plain, the smooth plain that will lead us straight to the sea?

"I see all that and much more. I see that each tank that they destroy us cannot be replaced and that, instead, for each one of theirs that they lose, three from France are put into operation. That's what I see.

One of Hagen's most distasteful characteristics is that he doesn't even lower his voice to make these demoralizing judgments. If someone were to hear me listen to you without protesting vigorously, they might believe that I participated in your ideas.

"Captain Hagen, I forbid you to express yourself in such terms!

"To order, Mr. Senior Tagger" he responds with a raspy tone of mockery.

I should reprimand him more vigorously, but then I notice that his gunner is painting three little American flags on the flank of his "Tiger".

"Three?" I ask.

"Naturally" he responds with insolent pride ". It was the least he could do in two days of combat, right?

Three tanks destroyed. And I know that Hagen doesn't lie. If your gunner draws a crashed and barred flag, it is because he has shot down an American tank, without a doubt.

I'm not envious, but I wish those three little flags were mine.

"I congratulate you" I say.

"Thanks.

For a moment we smoked in silence. A group of American prisoners passes before us, led by our infantrymen. In the distance you can hear the deep pulsations of the 88 mixed with the high-pitched barks of tank guns.

They are moving forward without us, but we will catch up with them as soon as we refuel. We won't be too late, I assure you!

The American prisoners, in column, with their long khaki cloaks, their steel helmets and their knitted hats, look robust and well fed, but their eyes reveal a miserable fear. These are by no means the heroes of the legendary Far-West and adventure films that pre-war Hollywood riddled us with. Rather, they look like the waste from the industrial neighborhoods of Chicago and New York.

"It's possible," he muses, throwing away the cigarette. For every one of our poor lads who take up the rifle for the first time now, or our weary Russian grenadiers, there are five like these.

"Captain Hagen!

"Mr. Commander Tagger!

There is really no reason to organize a dispute, which would lead to nothing. And Hagen seems up for a fight. Apparently an hour of inaction is enough for him to become the undisciplined wayward again.

Colonel Pieck calls us. I have to finish these pages.

December, 19.

Not vainly, because I have done nothing but fulfill my duty, but with legitimate pride, I head these lines with my new degree. The order has just reached me and I have received it from the lips of "Oberst" Pieck. I have been promoted.

Hagen too. Now he is older. I have congratulated him and he has answered me something about putting the braided epaulet on top of the cross when they pick it up. Naturally, I did not want to listen to you.

But let's go back to our story.

Oberst Pieck has given us the orders. Apparently, although of course temporarily, we are in detention. Ignore how, since the sky, completely covered with clouds, barely allows flight; a division of American paratroopers has managed to be planted in our path, right on our front line of attack.

They clarify it for me. They have taken her by land. That reassures me. Time is still our ally, then.

The fact is that they have blocked, as I said, our frontal attack. The paratroopers are in a city whose name resounds in me like a bell. Bastogne. I still seem to remember Hagen's long, strong index pointing at it on the map.

And there they defend themselves, like cornered rats. Of course, General Von Manteuffel immediately gave the order to continue on the sides to encircle the city and the paratroopers within it.

Our mission, Oberst Pieck has told us, continues: to reach the Meuse by all means at our disposal. And who doubts that we will fulfill it? Two of our divisions continue their advance, although apparently somewhat more slowly. We, I believe, are on a mission to destroy that obstacle that Bastogne represents.

Immediately after the conference with the colonel, which is attended by all the officers of the brigade, I have returned to my dear

"Tigre", in which I have not yet been able to paint a little flag, but which I will do if the help of God is still auspicious for me.

Hagen did not meet me until after an hour, which surprised me. But right now I don't have time to tell anything. They order us to move forward and we have to. Go ahead, then, and may victory cover us with its wings.

December, 19. Night.

Thank goodness I seem to have a little time now. I will use it to continue transcribing in this diary, which has made me so precious, the latest events.

Which have been abundant.

Bastogne has not fallen, despite our forecasts. But, let's go by parts. I have to put my thoughts and my memories in order. Because in a battle the soldier hardly sees more than what he has in front of his nose. Then a piece of information here, a piece of gossip there, taken at random, allows him to reconstruct what the general picture of operations has been.

First of all, I repeat: Bastogne has not fallen.

We have thrown ourselves upon it with all our might and encircled it. Yes indeed. The city is enclosed in a circle of steel, inexorably narrowing.

Through the fields that surround it, through the snow-covered forests, our armored troops and our brave grenadiers fight against an enemy whom we assumed to be weaker, but who resists furiously, perhaps with the courage that despair lends.

Bastogne is at a road junction. It is a key place, there is no doubt about it, and more at this time: when the Sixth "Panzer" and part of the Fifth are heading forward impetuously, followed by infantry divisions, by artillery, by impedimenta, flanked by Destruction engineers, sappers, miners, and supplied by a somewhat sparing quartermaster, we have to admit it, in honor of the truth. And more due to the fact that not being able to bomb ourselves due to weather circumstances "fortunately! "They have bombed our supply lines.

I had to attend the battle in one of the points of greatest friction: approximately three kilometers from the city, almost right on the border of Luxembourg, as I have seen on the map, between the two roads that from the East converge on the city. A great forest of dense trees, among which the Americans supported by antitanks, "bazooka" shooters and mortars have taken refuge.

For a moment it had stopped snowing. The flakes had turned into drops of water, and this led us to believe that it would be an advantage. Unfortunately this has not been the case. The water has frozen immediately, because the temperature is very low, and the chains of the tanks remain as if we were rolling on glass.

My tank, several times, has collapsed and has left our cannon pointed at our own troops. Immediately, Pieck gave the order to leave the road from which we were machine-gunned to go into the forest, whose youngest trees we uprooted. Fortunately there are practicable trails and through them we have infiltrated like water through a sponge.

I have had to destroy a nest of bazooka shooters, that dangerous British invention, which we should have invented ourselves. The blow of one of those torpedoes whose propeller handles two names, is something truly shocking, I have seen how at its impact a "Panther" split in two, gutted like a worm that a shoe found in its path.

I fired two volleys at him, once located, and watched with satisfaction how his servants flew through the air like rag scarecrows.

Behind me, on foot, come two companies of infantry, protecting themselves with my butt and my flanks. One look at their faces made me think maybe that damn monkey Hagen wasn't far off.

Many of them are quite old enough to fight on the front line, and others are youngsters who advance in leaps, wild eyes, tense bodies, who unfortunately miss out on accidents on the ground that would serve to shelter a complete squad and, instead , they use shelters where they are wiped out by snipers.

But I must not be discouraged by these impressions. If the High Command has decided to employ older and younger reservists, it must have had powerful and well-established reasons for doing so. There can be no doubt about it.

A little further, and always in the course of this dreadful afternoon, I have had to face an even greater danger.

Protected by a thick group of old trees with thick, frost-hardened trunks, the Americans have laid various mortars and ... something much worse.

The first mortals alert the infantrymen who walk behind me, and they deploy in guerrillas, swiftly, under the orders of their officers. I take the radio.

"I have in front of me the level five hundred and two, colonel," I say.

I immediately hear Pieck's voice. This excellent regimental commander seems to have a hundred mouths and a hundred ears to hear all the parts that we constantly riddle him with. He attends to all of them and gives the exact and timely order to all.

"It's your goal, Tagger.

"Yes, Colonel. I'm going to attack him.

"What's wrong, Tagger?"

He has realized that I would not bother to inform him that I am going to fulfill the assigned objective, and of whose mission I am perfectly imposed.

"Anti-aircraft, sir colonel"

"Destroy them, Tagger. Do you need help?

"I think not, sir colonel

"How many cars do you have there at the moment?

"Five, sir colonel. But I haven't been able to get in touch with Hagen. I don't know if they have destroyed it.

"They haven't destroyed it, Tagger. I'm sending it to you right now. I have needed it elsewhere.

So now he's no longer "my captain"? Now he's the irreplaceable one again, the man he steals from me to use when he sees fit. I'm about to smile, when the tank radio brings me the familiar voice:

"I'm going there, Tagger. Value.

Damn monkey. Value? You'll need it when you get your hand on it. He's my subordinate, right? I have the right to order a mission without it representing a call for help on my part.

The four chariots that I have left fire continuously on that nest; But apparently, the damned American mestizos have appropriated some defenses that we made previously and resist as if they had any chance of getting out of that situation.

If there is any weapon that I have learned to fear, almost as much as antitank guns and torpedo planes, it is the antiaircraft when, set to zero, they present us with their howitzers. The speed of fire of these damn artifacts is chilling. In a moment, they can place five explosive grenades on one of them which, although they explode on contact with the armor, sometimes go through it, and above all, they destroy the chains, the tower and the transmission.

Inside the tank we cough because of the smell of cordite. From my position, with my eyes glued to the viewer, I can make out the group of trees that surely hide a casemate of cement and steel. The trees are jumping one by one to the impacts of our cannons, while with the machine guns we sweep all the space that surrounds the objective to prevent the servers of the "bazookas" and the grenade and gasoline bottle launchers from showing their noses. .

"Ready" I hear in the headphones.

Hagen is finally here.

"Two AAs behind those trees.

"Well.

Well? I contain a curse. But this is not the time to dispute.

At that moment one of our cars is hit by a series of impacts. Culatea, almost reared like a horse and, rotated one of its transmissions, it remained flank, offering an excellent target for the Americans. It looks like a beetle that had all the legs torn off from one side. They immediately get fat on him.

"It seems impossible to attack that, right?" Asks Hagen, whose chariot is pulling to the left of the target. The other heads of machine seem to think the same as him.

I order that they be distributed among the trees. Yes, apparently it is impossible.

And at that moment I see a small group, three foot soldiers, stumbling forward. One of them carries a device on his back that I know well. A flamethrower. Those brave men want to help us, but they will never be able to get bare-chested.

"Understood," says Hagen, without my needing to say a single word to him.

And I see how your car starts running. For a moment its chains slide on the frozen ground, while its cannon spits furious flares. Then, anchored in a small mound free of snow, he picks up speed and heads like a cyclops towards the obstacle.

"Good luck" I say. And I order my gunner to add his fire to it until it covers with a jet of steel if I hide.

The Americans, for their part, have not stopped. They continue firing, but their firepower seems less. They may not have enough ammunition.

The three infantrymen stick to Hagen's chains and advance with him. They have understood. Hagen advances obliquely to protect them as much as possible.

I raise a prayer for them. It seems almost impossible, but I have seen Hagen do things as difficult as that.

It's coming ... it's coming ...

Suddenly, the tank turns on its butt at a twenty-five degree angle. It is a magnificent gesture. There you have it, boys, he seems to say.

The three soldiers interpret it and do not waste a second. Those aren't rookies, obviously. They have done it with the mastery of veteran soldiers

The one with the "flammenwelfer" points it out. Like in a movie I see the mouth of the sleeve that rises and, suddenly, the jet of fire, the horrible fiery finger that advances slowly.

We hold our breath. The Americans must have realized it too, because their shots are getting worse; but already the incandescent point is approaching them, crosses between the trees, which sizzle, and finally collapses with all its ardor on the blockhouse.

A tiny volcano erupts before our eyes. It looks like a fountain of fireworks, among the burning trees, and the ammunition packages that explode.

The obstacle is no longer so. I wait a few moments for the outbursts to subside and order to advance. With shouts of joy, howls of triumph, the infantrymen spread over the target like a flock of lobster.

I wipe the sweat. Hagen's voice reaches my ears.

"Clever. Tagger. The sweep is over. Go ahead?

"Go ahead" I answer.

But here I must interrupt the writing. I am falling asleep and the brandy, of which I have drunk almost a bottle, may be the fault that these pages are not the faithful and cold reproduction of what has happened this long afternoon. It has seemed to me that I have used some words, phrases, turns, somewhat emphatic. If I ever have time I will reread it, but I am not going to polish it. That would detract from his enthusiasm and, on the other hand, this is the diary of a soldier at a crucial moment in his life, not the account of a historian, as I have already noted.

No, I will leave it as it is, even with its possible lack of objectivity.

December, 20.

We really don't deserve this.

When I barely began my narration three days ago with exultant exclamations, nothing made me expect that I would have to moderate my justified joy after such a short time.

I reread the previous lines. Perhaps now I also let myself be carried away by a somewhat paralyzing pessimism. The situation may not be the way I see it now, with my eyes and brain tired from so many hours of almost uninterrupted combat.

I write it: It seems that we have been arrested. That our vigorous advance, our sweeping march towards the sea, has been slowed down by various factors, of which it is certainly not the smallest that time turns a hostile back on us.

Yes, I have no choice but to record it here. I would not be loyal to myself if I did not do so. But let's proceed in parts.

I stopped writing yesterday, still under the rejoicing rule of our victories. Those victories, oh, they weren't as big as me, a participant in them, they seemed to me. My eyes had been filled with destroyed, scorched blockhouses, crushed enemy tanks, forests thundering from the impacts of our artillery. That was only, unfortunately, the part that I had lived, not the general outline of the battle.

The arrival of the night brought us the rest, well deserved. We were given the order to stop the cars to make way for the new divisions that had not yet entered fire and to consolidate the positions taken from the enemy.

Coming out of the tank, my legs could barely support me. I was reeling like a drunkard! A cold ranch, with cans of meat still hastily affixed under their label, another advertising "Made in the United States" "supreme irony!", Coffee and brandy.

We devoured the meat until the tin was perfectly plucked, and we lit cigarettes. We were not given a supply of the latter, which makes me fear bitter days, deprived of something that is almost as important to the soldier as food.

We were in a clearing in the forest, near the road our convoys constantly passed by, constantly bringing new reinforcements to that hornace that is the front, and which consumes everything they throw at it.

We all would have preferred to sleep somewhere warm, in any of the conquered towns or villages; but unfortunately that is impossible.

Suddenly, the news. The brigade general summons the chiefs. We went, but when we met in a hidden farm under a thick forest of chestnut trees with the branches torn by shrapnel, I saw that if we were all there, then our losses were important.

"I just received news from the division," the general told us. He was sitting at a pine table, with a map on it. He looked at us with his sharp eyes, rimmed with red from exhaustion ". My lords, we have been assigned the mission of taking Bastogne.

There was a murmur, promptly silenced by the general's hand that rose into the air, flashing.

"The city hasn't fallen yet, I don't need to tell you. Surrender has been offered to General McAuliffe, commander of the paratroopers encased in it. His reply has been rude and unbecoming of a military man, but extremely graphic. I'll just translate it as "noses," very loosely, by the way.

"What do you expect, my general? Asked "Oberst" Pieck, whose face was caressed by a shrapnel helmet, producing a long wound that has not prevented him from continuing in his post.

"Wait for the weather to clear, Colonel. That is what they expect. As soon as that happens, and God forbid it is soon, his aviation would crush us. Unfortunately, the aerial protection that the Grand Marshal of the Reich promised us has not been able to become a reality.

Many eyes watched him intently. That was serious news, but fear could be read on no face.

However, I was startled. Hagen's elbow brushed my arm. What would this rascal want to tell me? Did he think his absurd fears could have the slightest foundation?

"So, my lords, we must take Bastogne if we do not want that accursed city to thwart our well-considered plans. I think I have made myself understand well.

No one nodded, but the general knew he could count on his men.

"I see" continued this excellent chief "that there are many clearings in your ranks. Tomorrow there will be more, I can assure you, because I have promised to the "Genealleutnant" that tomorrow we will take Bastogne or we will all perish in the effort.

Nobody likes to be told this, but we are soldiers and we understand perfectly when it is necessary to start saying goodbye to our skin. It had in our ears the death toll of a death knell. Hagen's elbow went back to mine. These were not times conducive to jokes or sarcasm.

"Sirs, I am not the bearer of good news, at least not very good. But I make you part of them precisely because tomorrow, when you face the enemy, I want you to know that you are fighting for something more than for a city, a village between roads in enemy territory, but that you are fighting for the German homeland, for the homeland of our fathers.

He paused dramatically. Only the continuous rumbling from the front interrupted the silence. Because there, in the living room of that Luxembourg farm, you could have heard the creaking of a woodworm.

"My lords, the SS 'Panzer' Sixth Army has seen its advance slowed in the vicinity of Krinkelt, and even though they are doing their best to break the 'impasse', according to my reports they have not yet succeeded. For our part, the outposts of our glorious Fifth Army have not yet achieved their goal of reaching Dinant on the Meuse, even though we have no doubt that we will. But, gentlemen, in order for the "Generalleutnant" to fulfill its objective, we need to take this damned city that opposes us so desperately. We cannot leave behind us a nest of well-armed and well-equipped soldiers.

We nod. That was on all minds.

So, gentlemen, take note of all my instructions. In the absence of some new event, all of you will faithfully follow them tomorrow, at three in the morning, when we will begin the frontal attack.

He got to his feet and slowly, slowly, but with a clear and precise voice, he gave us orders. When it was over, we saluted and retired to our posts. I walked along with Hagen, who, despite the cold, was smoking a cigarette with his bare hands.

"Tomorrow, then, dear, you will enter Bastogne or you will die," he said suddenly.

"" We will enter or die. "

"I do not.

I turned to him. Our footsteps sounded on snow and hardened earth.

"What are you saying?

"That the glorious Second Division, the mighty Third Regiment, the unbeaten Second Brigade, will have to do it alone. I can't help you.

"You're crazy!

"I'm not." Ulrich. I have been given another mission. Tonight I must report to Model headquarters.

I was dumbfounded.

"But, in the name of God, what are you going to ...?

"It is a military secret, Ulrich. But since you already know that military secrets are formulated to be broken, I don't mind telling you, because I know you are a good friend and an excellent German officer.

I was smiling. We passed the ranks of chariots, camouflaged in the forest, with the bows towards Bastogne, whose gleams we could see in the distance, reflected in the bellies of the low clouds. It was neither snowing nor raining, but it was very cold.

A soldier plaintively played the harmonica, and two or three, beside him, began to sing in low voices:

"For den Kaserne, for den Grossen Tor ..."

"Are you kidding. It's another one of your damn jokes. What other mission could you serve better than on "Katty"?

He lit another cigarette. In the light of the lighter I saw his face. He was not smiling. On the contrary, he appeared serious, extremely serious.

"No, Ulrich, I'm not kidding. Where did I spend three years just before the war?

I suddenly remembered. He had told me once. He spent some time, three years, in the United States. But what did that have to do with ...?

"Ulrich" continued with the same seriousness ", old comrade, the General Staff wants to blow up the bridges over the Meuse. He is going to send German soldiers dressed in American uniforms to infiltrate through the Allied ranks, with that mission. As you will understand, they need to speak English perfectly with an American accent. I am already one of those men.

"I already said. I understood.

"It's almost time to introduce myself. I have accompanied you here, but I am no more. Here we part.

"Who will send 'Katty'?

"Lieutenant Norr.

He dropped the cigarette and held out his hand. I shook it. Two soldiers, there in the cold night, clasping hands. Two friends.

"Goodbye, comrade.

"No," I said through a tight throat. " Goodbye, Dieter.

He turned and left. I lost sight of his greenish-gray cape.

A good comrade. A good soldier.

So many like him have been lost in this war ... So many ...

She mustn't think about him. He was going to fulfill his mission, and I had to fulfill mine. The soldiers continued singing, in low voices, impregnated with sadness and longing.

«Bi einst, Lili Marlen, bi einst, Lili Marlen ...»

At three in the morning we got into the cars and the brigade set out. Forward always forward.

December, 21. Early morning

As I said before, time is no longer on our side. The first thing I saw when I woke up from a heavy sleep was that the sky, which was foggy when I fell asleep, was now almost flat. I saw shreds of clouds and stars in the frosty early morning.

All of our eyes focused on those stars eagerly. If they continued to shine, if the next morning the sun showed its yellow face through the clouds, we would immediately have the enemy planes above us. We all knew what that meant.

But at that moment we had to carry out orders, with stars or without stars, with sun or without sun.

The first brutal, piercing attack brought us to one of the enemy's strongest points of resistance: the defenses that the American engineers had mounted hastily, but firmly, on the outskirts of the town.

Half a brigade managed to reach them, fighting an enemy who desperately clung to every accident on the ground, to every blockhouse, clung to the earth and the trenches dug in the stony ground by the frost, and left kill by responding to our fire with theirs, to our tanks with their "bazookas", their antitanks, their antiaircraft guns, their mines, their rifles and their hand bombs.

Between us, taking advantage of the smallest gap, the German infantry, the best soldiers in the world since the hegemony of Sparta, rushed in a torrent flooding those points that we could not reach.

What a battle! What a splendid battle! Odin would have been pleased with his sons if he saw them fight like that, without giving or receiving quarter, returning bayonet for bayonet, grenade for grenade, blow for blow, bite for bite.

But my hand bends, my pen falls. My eyes are invincibly closed, my heart beats irregularly due to being tired. Tomorrow I will continue, if tomorrow ...

December, 21.

Unfortunately we have not managed to achieve the objective that the general gave us. It is not our fault if we have not succeeded, and neither is it our fault to stay alive after failure. We have tried by all means to obey both orders.

We have thrown ourselves again and again against the American defenses, with redoubled courage, but we have always encountered fanatical resistance that forced us to retreat. Incredible, but I have to confess it loyally.

Our bosses have analyzed the situation exhaustively, they have looked for the weakest point to insert the attack wedges into it, but it seems that an adverse demon takes pleasure in breaking all our hopes, in violating our most ardent desires.

We have reached the first houses of Bastogne, we have had before our anxious eyes the headquarters from where the orders that oppose the German advance depart. Useless. With death in our souls we have had to retreat again, pursued by its intense artillery fire that crushes us, pulverizes us.

I know that reinforcements have been requested from the Führer's Headquarters, but those reinforcements have not yet arrived. The carts are less and less numerous, they lie on the roads and in the forests by the dozens, by the hundreds, turned into mountains of twisted iron. Corpses cover the hills with their thousands of frozen bodies. All in vain. In vain is this grim slaughter, this massive destruction.

Are we not, then, the chosen ones? Should I allow doubt to twist in my German chest? Are we to see how those American mongrels, those English traitors to their Germanic blood, trample the sacred Teutonic soil? No and a thousand times no!

But...

The 'Volkgrenadieren', the 'Panzer' divisions, both the pride of our Army, are exhausted. A body surrenders when the blood begins to lack in its veins, and that is what is happening to us in these bitter days that so bitterly, alas, began. An adverse fate is brewing on us.

And everything, why?

Only the strength of three divisions oppose our frontal attack. There are American paratroopers, belonging to the 101st Division, there are some infantry troops, engineers, gunners, but all of this in much smaller numbers than ours. Are we not going to be able to do now what four years ago would have been a leisurely military walk for our weapons?

I must confess it, even if only in a low voice and in this diary that, now I see, no one should read later, because what could have been a clarion call of enthusiasm has turned into a moan of bitterness. I must, I repeat, confess it: we cannot.

I will not fall for the topical excuse of blaming the weather, weather conditions, bad luck, our failure. To you, daily, I confess that sometimes I think that there has been something wrong in the plans that were formulated in the offices of the General Staff. But who am I, humble Oberstleutnant, to doubt the clear judgment of my superiors? Do they not have in their hands all the threads, all the information necessary to coordinate the best of plans? Don't they have the intelligence, study, acumen, and military science?

They have them, no one can doubt that, but ... what happened then? Is there no one who can explain it to me?

Today, twenty, we have made one last attempt. Regrouping our forces somewhat scattered by the last battle, we have risen to the assault.

Miraculously, and never better used the word, since it can be said that he has participated in all the combats, the thirty-three tons of my "Tiger" are still intact, except for two or three indirect hits. I forgot to say that I commanded the regiment, due to the death of the heroic Colonel Pieck, who fell bravely, hit by a direct hit, on his observation post. I do not know if I will get out of this alive, and I do not wish it very much, because if Germany falls, what will become of us, its defenders? What luck awaits us? But most likely the command of the regiment, which I now hold on a provisional basis, will become effective if the god of battles decides to turn his benevolent face toward us.

However, now is not the time to think about it, but to save Germany. Honors, rewards, time will have after arriving.

As I was saying, we have made a desperate effort. This is not understood! Deprived of supplies, locked in a circle of fire and steel, where do they get the courage, the ammunition, the supplies to continue resisting? There must necessarily be a general in front of us who would not detract from our Army. I can't find another explanation. Americans are not soldiers, like us, they are people hastily recruited in a country that lacks a war history and a General Staff condensed by nearly a century of military science.

Anyway, this is not my thing. I have my goal, which is there, opposite, in that city, just a town, which will surely go down in the annals of History. In Bastogne.

Our main objective is a well-fortified and cemented group of farms, in which American paratroopers resist, according to what the prisoners inform us.

They have deployed three heavily armored tanks, and they are the ones that respond to our fire when we manage to cut their forward lines, made up of groups of shooters with "bazookas" and two antitanks.

I order two of our "Tigers" to fire incessantly at the American tanks, while the real attack comes from the left, with my "Kind" leading the way. My faithful "Tiger" whom I love so much.

Three other tanks follow me, and behind, between us, moving in rapid zig-zags for cover, the grenadiers advance, their bags well laden with hand bombs.

We part the trunks of the felled trees, we crush the Phrygian horses, we roll over the cement posts driven deep into the ground, and we circumvent the anti-tank ditches into which if we fell we would be as useless as beetles on our backs, and finally we have before us. view the target. Miraculously, those farms have preserved their slate roofs, their gray stone walls.

Not for long, though. As the two "Tigers" continue their duel with the American tanks, we begin the bombardment, and the infantrymen spread out to cut off their supply from behind.

I think we are going to get it, we are about to get it. Hurrah!

We have achieved it!

American tanks cannot move, although they can fire. They are, in reality, a cuirass with a cannon. They have no more in sight.

The grenadiers have engaged the American resistance groups behind the farm. This is my first operation as a regimental commander and I have reason to be rightfully proud of it.

There are five farm buildings. From the first salvo, we managed to devastate one of them. The roof is blown up, its defenders rush out howling. Through the visor I observe how the clothes of one of them burn, and how he rolls on the ground to put out the fire that burns him.

They must have noticed our maneuver, because one of the tanks turns the long antenna of its cannon towards us and sends us a salute. Fortunately he has not had time to take aim and his grenade passes over my tower.

At that moment, the fire of our two "Tigers" destroys one of the American tanks. The other, unable to move, desperately defends himself, but his fire cannot against the converging jets of ours. It bursts into ink-black clouds, engulfing you in a moment.

I give the order to attack. Too late I notice our grenadiers retreating, splashing the wet stubble greenish-gray. Something must have stopped them and forced them to retreat later.

But, from where I am, I can be of little help to them. So go ahead!

We reached the stone fences that border the buildings, and by then we have managed to knock down two of them, reducing them almost to the walls. It is then that I realize what was preventing the passage of our brave infants.

An American assault group, soldiers dressed in khaki, with long cloaks, round helmets on their heads, and heavily armed are dispatched as they please. Protected by a barrier made up of sandbags, cement blocks and crisscrossing steel beams.

If we had had aviation, this would not have happened. She had warned us in time of the presence of that obstacle behind the farm.

Of course, fortunately, they don't have the help of airplanes either. I wouldn't want to see their torpedo bombers fall on me, chilling screeching of displaced air and spray me with ten-inch torpedoes.

The defenders of the farm retreat in disarray, abandoning their equipment, and the objective remains in our power. At least momentarily, since between the defenses our infantrymen were retreating from, the muzzles of two anti-tank guns appear, which begin to fire almost immediately.

I order the tanks to stay as far away from them as possible, interposing between them and those mouths that machine-gun the farm walls, and I report the situation to the division's headquarters.

The order is: resist at all costs there. Consolidate positions and ... resist.

To which I prepare. My tanks respond to the antitank fire by sticking out nothing but cannons above the half-ruined walls of the farm, and directed by the infantry observers. A brave feldwebel, with a portable radio, he guides shots, and we have the satisfaction of seeing his defenses diminish little by little.

I have to stop writing. I have been ordered to report to headquarters as soon as possible, three kilometers back. I give the appropriate instructions to Commander Jung, get out of the tank and get into a small car fitted with chains that is useful for cases like this.

December, 21. Later.

The division command has done me the honor of calling my modest feat a "goal conquered," and they are setting up a supply line to the farm. This fills me with pride because, although I have achieved little, few like this can be a great military victory. I am a grain of sand, but many grains make a mountain.

But, alas! I have also heard other news, much less pleasant. Our meteorologists tell us that the improvement in the weather is advancing rapidly and that perhaps tomorrow we will be at the limits of the anticyclone.

We all know what that means. Allied planes will be able to supply Bastogne, and their formations will rush down on us to sink us underground with thousands of tons of bombs.

The general communicates it to us calmly, without a single feature of his face altering. Such a boss communicates courage and faith to his men, but does not prevent them from thinking. And I think that if the weather clears, as it does foresee everything, our offense will turn into a disaster.

But the bad news does not end there. The Americans, from the South, from Luxembourg and France, are beginning to press on the left flank of our spearhead. At the same time, from the North, the English bite the right flank. If the troops of that old Montgomery fox, the only man Marshal Rommel had to bow his head to, and Cavalry General Patton's Americans join together, they will have locked us up, as we have Bastogne locked up.

After the conference, I must return to my combat post. God willing that in the end we can break the backbone of that city that has done us so much damage.

Lieutenant Colonel Ulrich Tagger, of the Second Regiment, Second Division of the Reichwehr Fifth "Panzer" Army, died on December 21, 1944, heroic in defense of an objective assigned by the command. He was posthumously honored with the first-class Grand Cross of Iron. The undersigned thus testifies in the same diary in which the great soldier recorded his impressions.

Rest in peace.

Signed:

Hauptmann Gottfried Jung.

SECOND PART

At Clervaux they gave him an American uniform, of a private, since that way, they told him, he could go more unnoticed than if he used one of an officer, and false documentation, although as perfect as possible.

In a room full of maps, a colonel pointed out their objectives point by point with a pointer.

"You have to memorize the exact places, to go to them without hesitation" he explained. They must arrive at the designated sites at exactly the same time, even though they will be going by different paths. We grant them a period of time that will be sufficient for them.

He paused.

"When arriving at the place and it is time, those who have managed to pass through the enemy lines will carry out the work without waiting for the delayed ones. Those who have not succeeded then, it will be because they are dead or have been taken prisoner. I hope all of you have understood the instructions well.

There was a general assent. Most of them were officers, but there were five or six soldiers, chosen for their perfect knowledge of English, which was going to be absolutely necessary for them.

Dieter Hagen looked at them. He saw the same determined, obstinate expression on all faces.

How many of these will return? He thought. But that was something that did not concern him much at the time.

He dressed in uniform in one room, along with the men who made up the group in which he was to perform. His objective was Givet, at the junction of the road from Namur to Reims with that from Wellin to Phillippeville, where the two meet on the Meuse. The bridges had to be blown up at dawn on the 21st.

The plastic charges and their detonators were handed over to them.

"If you are taken prisoner, try to make these charges fly, even if you have to fly with them," the instructor colonel told them coldly. We would not like them to fall into the hands of the enemy. We still do not know if they know its chemical composition or not, but, in doubt, we prefer that they do not take any of us.

They nodded.

They then sped off in a car to an airfield at a location Hagen could not locate. It was neither raining nor snowing, but the clouds were very low and the cold was intense.

They were handed the parachutes and a flight sergeant taught them how to put them on, how to jump when the pilot gave them the signal, how to fall to do as little damage as possible when reaching the ground, how to get rid of the parachute, bending it and burying it in soil.

The colonel gave them the last instructions when they were already inside the apparatus.

"You will be released at ten minute intervals in an area that extends in a triangle between Givet, Beauraing and Fumay. That area is occupied by Americans. You will mix with them as little as possible and, if you run into patrols, I will leave it to your intelligence and improvisation how to get out of the way. One thing I have to warn you: the Americans know that we have infiltrated people behind their lines, since this is not the first time we have done it. In the impossibility of discovering us, when they have a suspicion, they ask questions that a German finds it very difficult to answer. They are questions about details that only an American or a man who has lived in America for a long time can answer.

Hagen nodded. It was the logical answer. It is very difficult for a German or someone who has not lived "inside" American life to know who the husband of a movie star little known abroad is, or what color New York mailboxes are painted.

Then the colonel shook hands with them.

"Good luck," he ordered, more than he said.

And it came out. The propeller of the little plane had been rolling for a long time, to keep the engine warm. Now it began to spin dizzily. A moment later they took flight.

In the aircraft were seven men in addition to the pilot and a flight corporal.

Hagen looked at them. There was a lieutenant colonel of engineers who commanded the group, and others whose grades he did not remember.

For a moment, at the sight of the lieutenant colonel's tense features, it occurred to him that he should tap him on the shoulder and say, 'Comrade, leave the command to me. You need to relax, because otherwise you will do anything foolish. "

But he was in the army and that could have cost him a gun. He stared straight ahead and relaxed.

The plane was pitching into the clouds. A heavy silence, disturbed only by the roar of the engine, stretched inside. Nobody spoke. Only the corporal leaned toward the pilot from time to time to say something in a low voice.

After a quarter of an hour, the corporal turned to them:

"Ready. The first must be thrown out within three minutes.

The first approached the hatch. The corporal's hand was on the lever.

"When I count three, sir," said the corporal.

The minutes passed. They were all leaning forward, as if that way they breathed better. Only Hagen leaned back, his head resting on the wall of the plane.

Suddenly, the corporal's voice broke the silence.

"One two Three!...

He yanked the door open and the other jumped out. The corporal turned to the second:

"You sir.

The same operation. Hagen was the fourth. When it was her turn, she lunged, feet together, and quickly counted to three. They had already been warned that the plane would fly low, even though it meant a lot of exposure.

Then he tugged on the parachute ring, and the huge black silk mushroom opened above him with a sharp tug.

In the frigid air, he descended slowly, seeing nothing. The first news that he was approaching land was the whisper of the wind in the treetops,

He brought his feet together and fell onto his right shoulder. He rolled on the ground and stood up, drawing the parachute ribbons towards him, then stopped to escape.

Except for the distant murmur from the front, I heard nothing.

He stripped off the parachute, folded it without useless movements, but could not bury it. The ground was hard and would have needed a shovel. Fortunately, there were plenty of dry leaves, already half rotten from the rain.

He hid it under a pile of leaves and took the phosphorescent compass out of his pocket. If the calculations hadn't failed, he must be within eight miles of Givet. He could cover them before dawn. Then he still had the whole day, until the next morning, when he had to join the others.

I kept hearing nothing. Throwing a glance at the compass and watch from time to time, he started on his way. The place was perfectly well chosen. There was no road, except for a few roads between the launch site and Givet. Since the front line was nearly twenty miles away, he had a good chance of not running into columns of soldiers, bivouacs, or supply convoys, at least for what was left of the darkness.

The place where he fell was a forest of trees far apart. However, he smiled at the thought that he could have gotten hooked on any of them and continued like this until some patrol or peasant discovered him.

He had been walking for an hour when, suddenly, he heard noise in front of him.

He dropped to the ground and stood still, listening. A moment later he saw a faint light, perhaps a flashlight, about fifty yards from.

The voices of several men reached his ears, but he could not make out the words.

They approached. He took the pistol in his right hand and clenched the butt firmly. His pulse was steady, despite the fact that he had hardly slept for several nights.

Twenty-five meters, maybe. Now he made out the words

"... And I told her: look, girl, if you let me put my hand inside your blouse, I'll tell you if they are false or not, so you won't need to swear, which is a very ugly thing.

They were Americans. If they discovered him, it would be useless to tell them that he was too. He had no reason to be there, and the least that could happen to him was to be brought before his bosses. He wasn't up to it, with his plastic loads in the bag.

He raised his pistol, ready to fire.

She heard the sound of frost-stiff leaves, creaking as men passed by. Then the flashlight came back on.

"It's this way, Chuck," said another voice.

"No, more to the left.

"Look, don't waste us any more time. I tell you it's around here, and I have a gallon on my sleeve, and you have none.

"Well, if you're going to abuse authority ...

There was suppressed laughter. They were almost on top of him now. He heard the sound of their breaths and the clash of metal on metal.

Then they passed. Their voices were lost in the distance.

"... yes, but why can't you guess what the little fox answered me? He told me...

Hagen still waited almost five minutes. Then he got to his feet and continued on his way, tripping over the roots sticking out of the ground, and over the stones.

It was dawn when he reached the road. He had decided to do this because it would be much easier to find an explanation for the presence of a lone soldier on a road than in the field.

He passed a destroyed farmhouse as the first light of a leaden dawn began to cast darkness from the countryside. A dog barked furiously, but that was the only sign of life he found.

Then his feet made contact with the asphalt cracked by the passage of heavy vehicles and tanks.

The thunder of heavy-caliber guns behind him made him realize he was in the right direction. Began to walk.

He was not tired. Although most of the war had been spent in a tank, before the start of hostilities he had been an excellent mountaineer. The only thing that bothered him was the excessive hours without sleep, but that is something that sooner or later all combatants get used to.

He would have covered a kilometer when he heard the noise of an engine behind him. He listened carefully. Only one.

He stood by the ditch, next to the elm trees that often line French roads, and waited.

A jeep was speeding by, jumping over potholes. Hagen raised his arm and the driver slowed to his side. He was a small soldier, dark and wiry.

"What's wrong?" He asked. Then he seemed indecisive. " What are you doing here?

"I'm going to Givet," said Hagen, "I guess the springs on the car won't break if you let me get on it."

"Well, of course not, but what are you doing here? Of what unit?

"Of the fifth, of course. Look, if you're not going to take me as a passenger, you'd better say so. I have to get to Givet if I don't want to get in trouble it's the MPs

"What unit did you say?

"The fifth, are you deaf?

"-No, but, the fifth, of what? Well, go up. I'm in a hurry too.

He started the jeep, while Hagen joined him.

"Do not think that I am usually such a questioner, but we have been told that we have to be careful. MPs are very special. They behave as if we belonged to them by right of conquest. "Do this, don't do the other, buckle up that belt, it's not in your kitchen." A mess.

"Are you telling me?" Hagen growled.

"Where are you from?

"Frisco.

"Good land, but bad city. Hey, don't be mad, but give me Toledo, Ohio.

"Well, give it to you.

Hagen was looking to the sides of the road. The driver began to whistle through his teeth. Then suddenly he said:

"Do you have a cigarette?

"I was going to ask you precisely at this moment. I have run out, "Dieter responded instantly.

"Lucky bitch. The last ones I had I have exchanged for a few hugs to a Belgian woman who smelled like cows. Hey, take a look at what I'm saying: it smelled exactly like Ohio cows. Is this not a coincidence?

"It does seem like it is.

Hagen took his hand from his pocket, armed with the pistol, and put it at the soldier's side. He paled and stared at him with crazy eyes.

"But what,..!

"Brake.

"You've gone mad,..!

"Brake.

The soldier stopped when he saw Hagen's eyes.

"Get down.

"But...

Hagen hit him on the head with the butt. He didn't want to hit it too hard; but the fact is that the soldier fell sideways, with his head over the side of the vehicle.

When Hagen bent over him, he saw that he was dead. He had broken his skull.

"Bad luck," he said quietly.

He removed the documentation and dragged the body out of sight of the road. It wouldn't take long to find out, possibly, but by then he might be a long way off.

The dead man's wallet was kept. A quick glance at the papers told him that he had become Private Second Class James Collins of the X Signal Battalion.

He removed the insignia that he wore at the bottom of his shoulder pad, two crossed rays, and put it on himself. If he didn't bump into some of Collins's comrades, this might do the trick.

It would have rolled another two kilometers when it passed the first convoy. The first news he had was of two motorcyclists wearing armbands with the initials MP on their sleeves.

They made an imperious gesture for him to lie down. He obeyed, and one of the policemen dismounted. He carried a submachine gun hanging across his shoulder strap.

"Stay still there, boy. Things come behind. Papers?

Hagen took them out and handed them over. The man glanced at them, then looked up.

"What are you doing here? Who did you steal that "jeep" from?

Hagen tensed, but his knowledge of the Americans hadn't exactly been learned from books. That was the policeman's way of talking to anyone, suspect or not.

"I just stole it," he said. Well, when can I come through? They wait for me at Ten.

"They will have to win the war without you. Wait here. Do not move, because one of the things that comes there could leave you stuck to the road like a strip of paper.

They mounted the motorcycles and continued on their way.

Hagen waited. A few minutes later he heard the roar.

The earth shook, and the telegraph wires sounded like violin strings. Heavy tanks were approaching.

There they were. They rounded the curve at forty miles per hour, glued to each other, with such a small gap that if one of them braked abruptly they would nose in from behind. They were heavy tanks, and their servants had their heads sticking out of the tower hatch.

They glanced at him as he passed and one of them waved his hand.

Hagen counted twenty. Behind them, trucks loaded with troops, covered with thick tarpaulins, on the roof of whose baquets an antiaircraft machine gun was mounted. Seventy of these passed.

Behind the convoy came another pair of military police. He had to show the documentation to a corporal, and he told him that he could pass.

He arrived in Givet at ten in the morning, after encountering another convoy on his way, this one only of trucks. Before reaching the first houses, he was stopped by another MP at the checkpoint.

"Use the main road until the first sign" was the order you received. " Then turn left. Have you been on the front line?

Hagen shook his head.

"Good, go ahead. If there is a convoy, pull out on the first street. Do not stop at the intersection of "rue" Chanzy. There are some types for whom the signs do not appear to have been painted.

At the entrance to the city he saw the first French uniforms. Givet is the last town before the border. The "rue" Chanzy is the Dinant road, and at its junction with the one he entered, there were also policemen.

He had to leave the jeep. Some of Collins's colleagues might recognize him, and besides, a walking soldier might be paid less attention than a vehicle.

The streets were crowded with soldiers and civilians. He left the vehicle a little before the Café del Comercio. There were so many vehicles there that his would not attract attention.

Givet has two bridges over the Mesa. One of them is on the "rue" Oger, a continuation of the road by which he had come. The other, a little to the north, through which crossed a railway branch, laid to cut across the curve of the general line from Rochefort to Philippeville.

He walked until he reached the river and crossed in the Plaza de la República. Groups of American and French soldiers, wrapped in their cloaks, hurried through. The elms stretched their flaking branches skyward.

He crossed the plaza and glanced down at the river that slowly trickled to his right. He leaned against the parapet and gazed at the foundations.

Hagen's eyes narrowed. The command that had ordered the blowing up of the bridge must have known that this was an almost impossible task.

It would have taken a demolition squad and time, above all time, and security to get the job done. How to do it in a few minutes, and in the heart of a city full of soldiers?

He cursed under his breath. He broke away from the balustrade and continued along the bank of the Meuse to reach the other bridge, at the Dervaux quay. The railway bridge was less difficult because it was made of metal; but the question of the lack of tranquility remained unresolved. The Dinant highway passed alongside him, and that highway was continually traveled by trucks and US Army vehicles. Anyway, all this would have to be solved by the engineer officer, who was the specialist.

He cursed under his breath. I was terribly hungry. He hadn't eaten anything in over twelve hours.

Across from him was the Cafe Mallet, across the pier. He walked over to him and stepped inside. There, at least, it was hot.

"What is it going to be, Joe?" Asked the waiter. He was an old man with a bald head, trying to cover his bald spot with five hairs arranged in a semicircle.

Hagen saw that there were scones on the counter. He ordered coffee and several of them. As they were served, he looked at the cashier. She was a woman of about thirty-five, beautiful, with black eyes and a sensual mouth.

At the second look he gave her, the woman's lashes fluttered.

"It's very cold, isn't it?" He asked in a soft voice.

"Very much, Madame," Hagen replied in French, with a strong American accent. " Coffee is appreciated.

"Monsieur did not know this place?

"Oh yes, I have come once, but Madame was not there.

The woman was taking the hook. Hagen had removed his helmet, and more than ever he was glad that he had never followed the German fashion of shaving the hair on the sides of the head and at the nape of the neck. That would have revealed him instantly to French eyes.

The cashier was now looking at his head. Then he would look at her hands. Hagen knew by heart what women saw before and after in him; Then, finally, she would look him in the eye again. She did it promptly.

"Would you like to have a drink with me, Madame?" He asked. They had given him some American bills, one dollar and five dollars, probably counterfeit, when they delivered the clothes.

"I will gladly have a creme de menthe.

He helped himself and leaned across the counter across from Hagen. He looked into her eyes and then at her breast. She made a move to cover it up better, but left the gesture halfway.

"Where are you from, Monsieur?

From Toledo, Ohio. But that doesn't matter, does it?

"No, it doesn't matter," she acknowledged, smiling.

A military policeman, with his truncheon and his armband, appeared at the door.

"Hey boy, documents.

Hagen handed them to him, the policeman looked at them, looked at the owner, winked at her and said:

"If you make a fuss or get drunk, give us a call, Madame. We will get rid of it with pleasure.

He she left. Hagen gestured.

"Those damned ones won't leave us alone for a moment. Not even when we are having a quiet drink.

She poured him a glass of brandy.

"It's on the house," he said. It's true. As soon as a couple of boys have come into the cafe, one of those obnoxious guys shows up. And that's worse. He makes me court and does not want competition.

He leaned over to Hagen, offering him a larger helping of cleavage.

"But for good clients I have a quiet place behind me.

"I'm afraid I'm going to need it," Dieter said, reaching out and placing it on Madame's arm. Nothing better than that for him at the present time. A quiet place where you can spend the hours you have left, until the arrival of the set time. At that moment, someone entered the cafe, Hagen turned to the newcomer.

He went to the counter. He was an American soldier, but only in uniform.

He was actually the lieutenant colonel of engineers, the man who commanded Dieter's group.

Their eyes met for only a second. Then they both turned their heads, indifferently.

"A brandy" asked the newcomer in French, with a strong American accent.

"Come on, I'll show you," said the owner.

"Isn't your husband here?" Hagen asked quietly.

She laughed, but without answering, At that moment, the same MP who had entered earlier, poked his head out.

"Come on, boy, document," he ordered.

The German took a deep breath. He took out the wallet with the documentation they had been provided, and handed it to the policeman. He looked at it, turned it a couple of times between his fingers, and when the German reached out for it to be returned, he put it out of his reach.

"It is not in order. Come on, come with me and don't think about doing stupid things.

The German didn't even look at Hagen. Leaning against the counter, he was watching the scene, apparently indifferent, but tight as a guitar string, actually.

"But, look, agent ..." began the German.

"I said come. But if you want me to ask you differently ... "He raised the baton in the air.

Hagen knew well that he must not intervene. If they caught this man from their group, the blast could still be carried out, albeit with great difficulty; but if they caught both of them, it would get much more difficult.

"There is going to be a mess," said the owner of the cafe. " Come with me.

The German put his hand in his pocket. It was a quick gesture, but the MP was faster than him. He dropped the truncheon hard and malicious on his arm, and the other gasped in pain.

"What do you resist, huh? Now you will see, pig.

Hagen braced himself for the worst. If the lieutenant colonel managed to get to his explosives, the cafe would be blown up, and so would he. He wondered coldly if he could shoot the policeman to death, and he moved slightly from the counter. He had no desire to end up volatilized.

But the policeman was trained to fight soldiers who sometimes resisted him, especially if they were drunk.

He struck again with the baton, this time on the German's head, and the German staggered. He was still trying to rummage in his pockets. As the policeman raised the baton again, he managed to draw his pistol and fired.

The bullet did not hit the policeman, but it did infuriate him. Many times they had resisted him, but they had never tried to kill him.

He hit him again, viciously, while he raised the whistle to his mouth, and blew loudly to call out to his companions. The German fell to the ground, hunched over, swinging his legs.

Hagen turned to the owner.

"Come on," he said. This is going to get hot and you never know what will happen to you. They always manage to find us something to lock us up for.

The policeman had caught the German and was dragging him out of the cafe, continuing to beat him. Hagen told himself that he would never forget that face, red, beastly, while the arm moved like a plunger hitting the already inert body.

The owner led him through a back room full of drawers, barrels and bottles, to a small room at one end of which was a ladder that led to the top.

In this one was the house. A stretcher table, a purring stove, well stuffed with coal; chairs, pictures on the walls, and a window overlooking the pier and the railroad bridge.

"You'll be safe here, boy" she said. Wait a bit, now I'll be back.

Outside on the street there were whistles and the roar of engines. From the window, Hagen watched the lieutenant colonel being taken away in a police jeep.

The owner took almost an hour to return. When he did, he was carrying a bottle of brandy and another of creme de menthe.

"Now we can have that drink. A good stir has been made, God. That poor boy ... Police are the same everywhere. First they hit and then they ask. For that it was not worth it that they had freed us. The Gestapo's methods were no worse than what that guy has used on the poor soldier!

He paused, looking intently at Hagen.

"You had the papers in order, right?

"You saw me give them to the same policeman who arrested that one. On that side you don't have to worry.

I'm glad. Anyway, they won't come looking for you here.

Hagen reached out his hand, took the woman, and drew her to him. A moment later, the owner's juicy, well-painted lips were pressed against his. As he kissed her, he vaguely remembered Anne Wald, Pronsfield's "burgomaster." Ana was a little younger than this one, but I couldn't have said which of the two kissed better.

At noon she had to go down to the cafe to serve the aperitifs, since at that time all the sailors on the dock were meeting at the Mallet. The café kept the name of its owner who died in Arras during the German offensive in 1940, leaving Bernice a widow.

Hagen turned on the radio, softly, and listened to the Allied station, which was broadcasting the news bulletin. The defense of Bastogne continued, supported now that the weather was improving, by waves of planes. Bastogne had been supplied from the air for the first time since it was encircled. The German offensive could be terminated. The Russians continued to advance, in Italy they were also advancing. Hagen was about to close the radio when his arm stopped short. I was there. Several Germans had been captured who had the intention of committing sabotage in the allied rear. One of the prisoners had confessed. They were on a mission to assassinate General Eisenhower at his headquarters. Thanks to his statements, it was hoped to capture those who remained.

Hagen made no gesture. He closed the radio and lit one of the cigarettes Bernice had left him.

He wondered which of the men he saw with him, in that room in Clervaux, was the one who had spoken. The lieutenant colonel, perhaps? One of the young lieutenants, scared or tortured by the American military police?

He glanced at his bag on his side, which was lying in the corner of the room. There were enough explosives in it to blow up the house, the entire block, but not for any of the bridges. On the other hand, he alone, what could he do?

He smiled crookedly. Little, evidently. Getting killed, perhaps, but it didn't appeal to him very much. Dying while carrying out the orders he had been given was one of the many accidents an officer is exposed to during war. Dying just because, by an act of pride or foolish arrogance, did not suit his character.

Well, whatever it was, that was over. He took the emblem of the signals corps, or the division, from the upper part of his sleeve, I did not know, because the American emblems changed with stupid frequency, and threw it on the stove.

Now he was a soldier who could belong to one division as well as another.

He couldn't leave now, because Bernice would see him walk through the cafe and ask him questions. She had been so satisfied with his behavior that she would not let go of him without trying to hold him back, or she did not know women. On the other hand, he wasn't in much of a hurry yet.

She came up at half past two. She hugged him and kissed him, calling him her "petit cochon americain," and he kissed her back with a certain coldness.

"I have to go," he said.

"So soon, « chéri »?

"Of course. You wouldn't think that I was going to stay here to wait for the end of the war, would you?

"Chéri" wouldn't be a bad idea. Coffee needs the arm of a man, a man like you. It's good business, but you need a boss.

"But General Eisenhower needs my arm too, so we're not going to argue any more.

But will you come back?

"Ah, yes, of course. If they don't take me elsewhere, you'll have me here tomorrow for the apéritif.

"Then,..

She kissed him again, leaving a crimson stain on his lips, which he then carefully wiped clean.

At last he was free of that octopus. He grabbed his camping bag and went downstairs. There were still several customers in the cafe, most of them French, who looked at him resentfully. They knew where it came from But none of them said a word.

At last he found himself in the cold street. A pale sun, the sun that had allowed the Allies to use their aircraft a hundred kilometers to the east, at Bastogne, shone in the gray sky.

He did not hesitate for a single moment. It could not head eastward, even if it was the shortest distance from the German lines. He had to make a detour, perhaps re-enter Luxembourg ...

"Luxembourg".

He was about to laugh. There was someone there who could help him. He was in danger, of course, but no less than if he were detained there and linked to the saboteurs. They would not forgive him, of course. That idiot who had said that one of his missions was to assassinate the general-in-chief of the Allied Army had sentenced them to death if they were caught; of that he had no doubt. By the way, where would that have come from? Or was it just one of the many lies the

Allies used in their propaganda services? Either way, he had no desire to find out now.

The streets were still full of soldiers. He didn't attract attention; But neither did he want a military policeman to see him pass him several times and recognize his face. The loitering soldiers, without being a rare item in the rear, did not deserve the approval of the military gendarmes.

Down the "rue" de Notre Dame he descended rapidly until he found a crossing for Oger, the road by which he had come. He walked along the sidewalk, under the protection of the overhanging eaves, with a brisk step, as if they were waiting for him somewhere. When he reached the canal, he dropped the bag, after having taken out of it everything that was not the explosives. The bag immediately sank. If some pinnace tripped over her, she would go to hell. If not, it would remain in the slime at the bottom until it fell apart.

Collins's "jeep" was where he had left it. He got on it and checked the gas. The tank was almost full.

"Good," he murmured. Now or never.

He put the jeep in gear, and waited. He didn't have to do it for long. From the intersection with the Dinant highway a convoy of trucks arrived, in line. There were five of them, and they were heavily laden, but not with troops, since only crates could be seen through the gap left free by the rear tarpaulins.

He stood next to the last truck and obediently followed it. On leaving the city the convoy stopped at the checkpoint. The MPs looked at the drivers' papers and made an arm signal. Hagen followed them and no one asked him.

The convoy continued along the second-order road, lined with signs in English indicating that this was the road to Luxembourg, and in many cases mysterious signs, which Hagen imagined would correspond to the locations of the various units.

At four in the afternoon they passed through Wellin and at five through Libramont. At the entrance to each of these towns there were military checkpoints, but all of them passed them without any of the military police officers wondering whether or not that "jeep" was included in the vehicle lists that the drivers presented.

At Neufchateau, Hagen had already made friends with one of the drivers, an Italian from California who had long lived in Frisco. When Dieter told him that he was traveling with them because it made him feel safer and that he was going to Luxembourg to find his colonel to meet him, the Californian told him that he could go with them, because fortunately the guy who was commanding the convoy was not a officer, but a sergeant, and that most of the time he was drunk, although with wide eyes and sitting on the bucket.

He invited him to dinner and they both celebrated with laughter that the cargo the convoy was carrying were bathtubs for the WACs of the female auxiliary services, who did not trust European bathtubs, or in general anything that had seen the light of Europe.

At seven in the morning they entered Luxembourg.

He had succeeded. At least he had achieved half of his purposes.

The school was situated on Palatinate Street, in a large brick building with a slate roof, and the municipality had built behind it, for the teachers, small houses surrounded by tiny gardens.

Dieter Hagen pushed his helmet forward. He went to one of the little houses, opened the gate, crossed the garden. He knocked on the door.

A sleepy voice answered him after a moment, asking what he wanted at this hour. Dieter didn't answer, and at last the door opened a few inches. A rosy face, with blond hair framing it, appeared in it. With a slow, deliberate movement, Dieter raised his helmet so that she could see his features.

The woman's eyes widened and then her mouth.

"Don't yell," Hagen ordered, putting his foot between the doorway-". It's me, but don't yell.

He pushed slightly and entered. He leaned against the door, smiling.

But ... Dieter! OMG!

The young woman's eyes looked at his uniform. Slowly he brought his hand to his mouth.

"Dieter ..." he repeated in a muffled voice.

"I need you to stay for a few hours" said the German reaching out his hand to her "I need it, Gerda. I guess you won't fail me.

Gerda Rosenkrantz was one of the teachers at the Luxembourg municipal school. She was twenty-five years old and had a body that would have made a lot more money in any fashion house. However, as she had assured Dieter many times, while he laughed, she had a real fondness for teaching. She wanted to become a professor of art history, and she studied for it while stripping cobwebs from the brains of small savage sons of miners.

"Dieter ... what are you doing in an American uniform?

"Hide me" he replied smiling. Gerda, are you going to keep me here for a long time? I have not eaten anything for several days.

He took her hand, drew her close, and pressed his mouth to her ear.

"Are you glad to see your captain, Gerda?

He picked her up in his arms and turned her around. Then he put it down again.

"You have something to eat?

She pulled away, looking at him, not daring to even believe what she saw. During the five months that Dieter spent in Luxembourg, with his division, they had been lovers. Of course, then the Germans were occupying the Principle, and the inhabitants of it, without being frankly Germanophiles, at least were not much opposed to them. But now the Americans were the ones occupying Luxembourg.

Dieter's gaze hardened perceptibly.

"You are thinking that this represents a conflict for you, is it not, Gerda? Is that what you are thinking right now?

"No, no, Dieter; I assure you not. But ... it was such a surprise, to see you appear, suddenly, and dressed in an American uniform ...

"I came only because here I was closer to the German lines, to which I want to return. I have been taken prisoner and I have escaped. But if you can't help me ...

"Wait," she begged, looking at him with her blue eyes. " Wait, Dieter, it was the surprise ...

Suddenly she fell into his arms.

"Dieter, how much I have missed you! You can't guess what I've cried thinking about where you would be all this time!

He stroked her hair, thinking quickly. He couldn't stay long in that house. All the more, until the night, since sooner or later his presence would be discovered.

"What time do you have to go to school?" He asked.

"The school doesn't work. Classes won't start until next month ... next year, of course.

"Better, Gerda, all I need is some food, if you have it, and a little information.

- "I have food," she replied. Oh, Dieter, to see you like that, like that, hunted ...! Poor Dieter!

Hagen smiled. The girl's body was glued to his. Their breaths mingled. He pushed it away and looked at it.

"You are as beautiful as ever, Gerda. I suppose American officials have told you many times.

"Shut up. I'm going to fix you something to eat.

He stopped for a moment.

"You plan to leave, of course. How are you going to do it?

"I haven't decided yet, but I'll find a way to do it. Do not worry.

"Maybe if I could get some civilian clothes ...

"Not. These are much safer. I have to go back there, Gerda, and a civilian couldn't get anywhere near the front line. They would stop him right away.

She went into the bathroom, combed her hair and washed her face and hands, while Hagen watched her, leaning against the doorframe, wondering if she had been reckless. How did he know what the girl was thinking after ten months of absence? Hadn't his feelings changed? After all, there had been some criticism from the other teachers when they saw her with the handsome tank captain of the invading army.

Then Gerda prepared a meal consisting of eggs, bacon, and potatoes. Hagen sat down at the table and ate hungrily.

When he finished, she handed him an already lit American cigarette.

"Are there many troops here?" Hagen asked.

"Many" she looked at him ugly, almost without blinking. To another man, that look would have been a bit annoying. He was used to women looking at him that way.

"American, I suppose?"

"Yes, and some French, although few. But...

"Are there tanks?

"We have seen many pass, but I don't know if they will be in the city. But, Dieter, I can't give you information. You are ..., you are from the enemy.

Hagen smiled as he blew a plume of smoke toward the ceiling.

"I am not asking you for military secrets, Gerda. Just general information. I need to know where I'm going to go.

She leaned on his shoulder. Through the thick cloth robe, the warmth of her body came to him. He hugged her tightly, with his left arm.

"I'm going to stay here until the night, if you don't mind.

"Care... me, Dieter?

"I need a bathroom. It seems to me that I have not bathed in ... centuries.

"You will be tired, right?

Dieter wasn't, but he didn't get her out of her mistake. A woman does anything for a tired and hungry man, especially if that man has been to her what Hagen had been to Gerda. There was no harm in his assuming he needed her.

"No one will know that I am here," he said. I will not compromise you. I suppose you have had difficulties with the direction of the school because of us.

She shook her head.

"Some, but everything happened quickly. People are too happy because they have freed us to think about all that.

"Freed from what?" He asked.

"Well ... of you.

"Bah, you are as German as we are, even if you put your street signs in French.

She kissed him hotly. And in that moment Hagen realized that he was tired. It was as if all the fatigue accumulated during a week of nervous tension had suddenly collapsed on him. His eyes were closing.

He fought the torpor, struggling to keep his eyes open. It was hard work for him to do it.

Gerda noticed this and ran her hand through her hair several times, accentuating her dream. Hagen got to his feet.

"Can I take a shower?" He asked.

She smiled at him. Her eyes were bright with tears.

"Why don't you sleep a bit earlier? You are going to fall asleep in the bathtub.

Hagen realized that it would be so and allowed himself to be led to bed. It was still warm from the heat of the young woman. He took off his boots and lay down. A moment later he was asleep.

He woke up, startled, and looked at his watch. Eight. Had he not slept more than half an hour? But when he saw the light on, he realized that he had slept for twelve hours straight. He stood up. I was fresh and rested. The young woman entered. She came dressed for the street and carried a package in her hand.

"I have gone out for a moment to buy some things to eat" he said "-. You've spent the day sleeping.

"Yes.

He took a bath, which took almost an hour. Then she made him dinner.

"Stay until tomorrow" he said with his mouth very close to his ear, in a low voice. Hagen laughed hoarsely and shook his head.

"Impossible. By day it would be much worse. Do you know if Bastogne has fallen?

"No," she replied sullenly. " You have not managed to take it. The Americans say they will release her in the next few hours.

Hagen stood up and buttoned his cloak. He looked down from his height at the Luxembourger.

Goodbye, Gerda, and thank you for everything. If we're both still alive, we'll see each other after the war is over.

"You're hateful," she said through tight lips. " You are an absolutely hateful being, and without heart, and without sentiment ...

Hagen kissed her and the last syllable was lost. She wrapped her arms around his neck, resisting letting go. As gently as possible, the commander disengaged himself.

"Goodbye, Gerda" he repeated. Please go out and tell me if someone passes by on the street. I do it for you, understand.

She obeyed. She turned her face toward him.

"No one.

She kissed him one last time and Hagen stepped out onto the cold street.

The jeep was where he left it, but it had only gas left for more than a few dozen kilometers and he couldn't think of refueling. Well, they would last as long as they did.

He climbed into it, took one last look at the girl's house, shrouded in the shadows of darkness, smiled slightly, and started the engine.

Now came the most dangerous part of all. Get closer to the front.

He supposed that there would be American military checkpoints at the exit of the city on the road leading to Ettelbrück, so he took the Rippig road towards the German border.

There was also a control in this one. Next to him, several dozen Army trucks waited for reviews. Realizing that it would be crazy to try to pass him with his vehicle, he left it on a deserted street due to curfew, and walked towards one of the trucks, the last one.

He was smoking a cigarette, calmly. A soldier from the supply service beckoned to him.

"Give me fire, will you?" - he asked. As he lit his cigarette, he looked at Hagen. " How long do you think we have here? Do you know something?

"No more than you.

"God, I'm freezing. I just had a cup of coffee, but it looks as if I have thrown it on the floor, judging by how little effect it has on me. I'd give anything for a drink.

The line started, and the man ran to his place, next to the driver. Hagen didn't even think about it. Jumping up, he climbed onto the back of the truck and, moving cautiously, stepped over the boxes until he was close to the bucket. There, he crouched down.

About a quarter of an hour passed until the truck began to roll down the highway, at about thirty miles per hour. Each turn of the wheels brought him closer to the Moselle or the Our. He had an irresistible urge to smoke, but he couldn't.

The rattle of the truck lulled him slightly, despite the twelve hours that he had slept. He woke up abruptly, when his head hit a drawer.

A formidable roar reached his ears. Tanks were passing by on the road.

He moved to the back of the truck and peered through the ties in the tarp. Indeed, huge masses crossed before his sight, and close, very close, sounded the roar of artillery. It was only a few kilometers from the front.

He jumped up and found himself at the edge of the wagon.

There were many soldiers getting out of the trucks, while the officers ran from one place to another giving orders as if they had gone mad.

"Soon! Get rid of that obstacle! Put them away!

Hagen mingled with them, joined by a line of soldiers trying to push aside a truck that had driven both wheels on one side into a deep pothole in the ditch. Meanwhile, the tanks continued to pass towards the North At that moment, a grenade exploded very close to where Dieter was. He ducked automatically, and beside him he felt the muffled groan of a man who had just been wounded. Then the wounded man screamed endlessly. Hagen broke away from them and into the field. Groups of soldiers were running from one side to the other, and it seemed to the German commander that they hardly knew what to do.

Hagen joined one of the groups heading north. It was made up, as far as he could tell, of engineers. Among them were many blacks.

As he walked behind them, several flares were lit on the horizon. The group stopped, while the officer yelled for them to continue. Above them they heard the noise of jet engines.

A caterpillar car pulled into the field behind them. The explosions of the bombs sounded closer and closer.

Hagen wondered if it was just a bombardment or did it mean that the front was very close, which he wanted with all his might.

The flares continued to illuminate the night with cold white light. In its glare he could see the faces of the American soldiers, with tense features, wide-eyed. It was strange to see the eyes of the blacks, in the middle of their dark faces.

A grenade fell very close to them and they all threw themselves to the ground. Then a voice began to shout that tanks were approaching.

If it was a German advance, Hagen, amid the darkness and nervousness of combat, could not identify with his own. He began to think that it had been a bad idea not to wait until morning to try to jump to the other side.

The soldiers did not back down. Their officer, who almost always marched ahead of them, yelled hoarsely that they had to get a line ahead. They continued, after the brief hesitation of the bomb.

They must have approached the road again, because they heard the heavy tanks passing by it again. All was noise, confusion and darkness except when the flares descended slowly from the sky, filling everything with moving shadows.

Hagen stumbled upon a fallen body, probably a dead body, and continued, always on the heels of the soldiers. The entire horizon lit up with the explosion of the grenades, as if it had caught fire. It was fought, and not far from there.

Finally, after almost an hour of mind-boggling march, they came to a place with low stone fences. They jumped them and found themselves in what looked like a farm yard, where there were more soldiers. The officer who commanded the group approached another, whose lapels was an oak leaf.

"At your command, Commander," said the engineer officer. We bring the barbed wire.

"Damn the lack that it already does, and cursed the lack that they had given such an order" replied the other shouting, his face decomposed. What we needed were tanks and "bazookas," and I don't think you guys bring them in a two-inch-tall cart.

"No, sir," replied the officer.

"There are tanks behind those houses. No, you can't see them, until we fire more flares, but the fact is, they've been machine-gunning us two hours ago. See what they can do with the materials they bring and what they find there. We have to prevent those tanks from reaching the road and cutting off the convoys or slowing them down. You don't understand me, you idiot? Move your legs!

"Yes sir. Boys, to work!

A flare exploded in the sky above them, and he descended on his little parachute, illuminating everything. Hagen looked ahead for a moment.

This farm was not isolated, but was part of a group of them. Behind the last one he saw the familiar cannons of two or three "Tigers" moving slowly to the left. Then they started shooting, and he fell to the ground.

The "Tigers" shots hit the farm twice, the walls of which were still standing, piercing them as if they had been made of mud. An acrid cloud of dust and plaster made him cough.

"Stop those tanks!" Yelled the oakleaf officer. Stop them!

But apparently there were no antitanks there, no "bazookas." The officer beckoned, and a soldier, armed with a portable radio, hurried over to him. The officer began to call insistently, while cursing. He called XV 34, and when they finally answered him, he said that there were several German tanks in between, that if they had forgotten that they had been saying it for two hours, and that the colonel would come in person to touch the guns of the German tanks if he doubted it.

Hagen smiled. He had realized that the tanks weren't trying to attack the farm head-on, but were waiting for something, maybe reinforcements, because what they were doing was pacing back and forth, while shooting, when in fact it wouldn't have been much work. sweep the buildings.

He understood what he had to do, and he did it without wasting a minute.

As nobody noticed him, nor expected him to do anything, he walked away, protecting himself with one of the corners of the walls.

He folded it, and found himself at the front of the farm. He stood still for a moment, as the flare died, and he heard tank bullets pass overhead, stirring the air with sinister screeches. Hearing them made him understand that the tanks were not firing at the farm now, but had raised the angle of fire, to fire "behind it."

That could only mean one thing: infantry forces were approaching

If they caught him there, in an American uniform, it would be useless to shout that he was a German commander. They would stick a bayonet into his body and continue their advance. So he did the only thing he could do right now: drop to the ground and stay completely still.

That he was not wrong was shown by the fact that no flares were lit again for a moment. The officer with the oak leaf on his lapel must have noticed that too, because he heard him yelling behind him, calling for lights and ordering his men to be careful, that this was a bloody trap.

There was a tense wait. Almost five minutes.

And suddenly, looking under the visor of the helmet, without lifting his head from the ground, he saw a bundle appear before him, leaping over the walls of the farm. Another, two more, five, ten, followed him.

They were leaning forward, rifles in hand, but Hagen could already make out their square helmets. Germans, they were Germans.

It did not move. The first rifleman passed him, walking like a wolf, and approached the corner of the wall. Two others, carrying between them what must be a mortar. They emplaced it in a moment, while the place was filling with soldiers, and they launched the first projectile.

Hagen remained motionless. He listened to the noise, which the Americans were making behind him. He had a German soldier next to him, so close that he could smell the acrid smell of his clothes, wet and sweaty. He was a rifleman who stood almost as still as he.

Then the soldiers advanced, no longer taking care to hide their presence. But more followed behind them, and at the same time, the tanks began to move.

He heard the commanding voices of a German officer shouting for the soldiers to circle the building, and the crackle of riflemen and machine pistols.

He risked raising his head slightly. German infantrymen passed by, crushing everything with their boots. The tanks had directed their march to the left, and one of them was launching projectile after projectile at the Americans.

It was at this moment that he risked sitting up, expecting any moment to feel the steel between his ribs. But he had seen an officer's white epaulettes gleam, with gold nails.

"Captain!" He called.

The officer did not hear him and Hagen repeated the call. The other turned to him and pointed the gun at him instantly.

" Do not shoot! Major Hagen from tanks on special mission!

The officer fired and the bullet buried itself next to Hagen's head, thanks to the fact that Hagen had moved quickly.

"Do not shoot! I'm German! Major Hagen from the tanks!

The officer] kept pointing at him. Then he barked a quick order, and two soldiers stood beside Hagen, bayonets two centimeters from his nose.

"Take him back.

Hagen got to his feet slowly. A new wave of soldiers appeared over the fence. The shots sounded more distant. They must have finished off the farm's defenders by now.

Bayonets jabbing at him, Hagen strode to the fence. T] captain had approached. His eyes coldly searched Dieter.

"What are you saying, dog?" He asked.

Hagen put his hands on his helmet and was immediately punctured in the kidneys.

"I just want to take it off," he said. I'm Major Hagen, on a special mission behind enemy lines. If there is any superior officer among you ...

"I am enough for what has to be done with you. Come on, guys, take it back. And if he tries to escape and you kill him, I won't be the one complaining. Back with him!

An officer with braided epaulettes and a golden nail in them, arrived. He had lost his helmet or taken it off and his blond hair hung in the air.

"What are you doing here, Borst? -" he asked the captain. Why don't you stick with your men?

"That American says he is German.

"I am Major Hagen, Lieutenant Colonel" Dieter repeated for the third time. Second Brigade, Third Regiment, Second Division of Major General Schlechter, Fifth Army "Panzer" ... "Generalleulnanl" Von Manteuffel.

The lieutenant colonel listened to him with his eyes fixed on him. Was very young.

"Bring him.

They led him to the rear. One of the tanks was stationary and its boss's head was poking out of the hatch. A flare ghostly illuminated his features.

"Lieutenant! Listen to this man ...!

He couldn't finish. The man peering through the hatchway stared at Hagen.

"Captain!" He exclaimed.

"Major" Hagen replied smiling.

"Do you know him?" Asked the Infantry Lieutenant Colonel.

"Yes, Lieutenant Colonel. It's the chap ... it's Major Hagen, from the Second Division.

The lieutenant colonel smiled.

What lightning and thunder were you doing there, in an American uniform?

"Special service, sir. I must see my superiors immediately.

"It's okay. I'll have them take him back. But the lines are very confused. The front seems very fluid to me.

He held out his hand and shook it. Then he ran after his men.

Hagen continued walking. For his pleasure, he would have gone up to the "Tigre" from which the tanker lieutenant greeted him, but first he had to go report. Damn reports, fifty times damn, especially when they are to announce bad news.

"Do you have a monkey?" He asked the lieutenant. I can't go through our ranks in these clothes.

Under the gaze of the two soldiers who had guarded him, and that of the lieutenant, he took off his khaki cloak, tunic and pants and, shivering in the cold night, put on his overalls. One of the soldiers handed him a cloak.

"Come on," Hagen said.

He looked behind him one last time, to the front. A slight tic twitched his right cheek. After everything he had seen in the Allied rear, he knew that this German offensive would probably be the last blow of the Reichwehr. The last.

It was not possible. There were too many men, too many tanks, too much artillery, too much of everything. It was enough for him to look at these soldiers that surrounded him, skinny, like hawks, emaciated, whom only patriotism, will, supported, and compared to those other robust, well-fed GI's ...

Yes, it would be one of the last German offensives, if it wasn't the last.

Then, with a firm step, he headed for the waiting car.

END